MW00931535

THANKSGIVING TREACHERY

A HOLIDAY COZY MYSTERY
BOOK SEVEN

TONYA KAPPES

TONYA KAPPES
WEEKLY NEWSLETTER

Want a behind-the-scenes journey of me as a writer?
The ups and downs, new deals, book sales, giveaways and more? I share it all! Join the exclusive Southern Sleuths private group today! Go to www.patreon.com/Tonyakappesbooks

As a special thank you for joining, you'll get an exclusive copy of my cross-over short story, *A CHARMING BLEND*. Go to Tonyakappes.com and click on subscribe at the top of the home page.

Thanksgiving Treachery

"Help! Please, someone help!" Our conversation was shattered by a bloodcurdling scream, unmistakably Mama's.

Darren and I exchanged a glance of alarm before racing out of the dining area, our feet pounding the tile floor. The echoing scream seemed to come from the hall leading to the delivery entrance. We burst from the hallway and into the vicinity of the entrance's staircase, where we found a horrifying sight.

Mama stood there, her face pale, her trembling hands covering her mouth. At her feet lay Albert Harden, the kind man who had delivered milk to Holiday Junction residents for as long as I could remember. His body was crumpled awkwardly at the bottom of the steps leading to the loading dock. From where I stood, it looked like a tragic accident, like he had slipped while descending the steps to his delivery truck.

"Oh, Albert," Mama sobbed, her voice quivering. "I just came out to check on a delivery and... and there he was."

Darren moved quickly to Albert's side, checking for a pulse, while I took Mama into my arms and tried to soothe her racing heart.

"It's going to be okay, Mama," I whispered, though I wasn't sure of that. I took out my phone from my pocket and dialed 911.

"911. What's your emergency?" the operator asked.

Darren looked up, his expression grave. "He's gone, Violet."

A cold shiver ran down my spine.

CHAPTER ONE

"To-furky," Millie Kay, my mama, harrumphed. "Who on earth ever heard of that?"

Her Southern twang garnered a snicker from Darren Strickland.

I glanced up from the list of activities I'd been curating, not as the *Junction Journal's* editor in chief, my newest title, but as Holiday Junction's secret Merry Maker.

More correctly, I was the co–Merry Maker with Darren, but the title might'swell have been singular. He'd had his nose stuck in that book of his since he'd decided to go back to law school and start lawyering around here. That left me with the tasks involved in the centuries-old sacred job of deciding where in our little town each holiday's final hurrah would take place.

"You told me I could invite friends who lived in the art district," I reminded her, getting a smile from Darren, though his eyes were still laser-focused on the book in hand. "And I quote." I lifted a finger and said in my best Millie Kay voice, "'Now, Violet, I don't want anyone feeling left out for Friendsgiving. You go on and invite all them people up in the mountain and ask them what they like to eat so they can enjoy a nice friendly sit-down.'"

Mama had bought the old run-down building and had a grand idea of turning it into what she called a Leisure Center. Technically, the place was a senior citizen building with activities like bingo, line dancing, and now knitting classes—thanks to Amelia—as well as painting classes—again thanks to Amelia—among other pursuits mainly for people Mama's age.

Now Mama wasn't too old, but she was old for a mother when she had me, and that made her feel much older than her actual sixty-something years on this earth. She was Southern to her core, carrying the region's traditions with her in her personality, and that, my friends, truly made her an old soul.

Like with most things Mama did, she brought the color into any situation here in Holiday Junction.

"I thought they liked to eat turkey, stuffing, gravy, sweet potato casserole, buttermilk biscuits, cheesy grits, hash brown casserole... you know." She sighed as she picked up and shook the list of food Amelia Hartman had given me when I asked her for one. "Good food. Stick-to-your-ribs food. To-furky." She wadded up the paper and stood, tossing it in the trash can as she walked out of the dining hall and into the hallway. "I've got a meeting with Marianne Drew this afternoon. She's trying to move the Mistletoe Masquerade Ball and might rent the Leisure Center."

"Don't worry about the wadded-up guest list. I've got a copy," I said, smiling when she acted like she didn't hear me. She heard every single word I said and was no doubt off to find the fixings to make a Tofurky. But I was glad that she might get her first big rental out of Marianne Drew, a local woman I didn't know but who had already sent in information for me to do a big write-up in the *Junction Journal*.

I knew her by name but had never been face-to-face with her. In fact, I'd gotten another message last week from the desk of Mayor Paisley, asking if I could come to the last event of the Thanksgiving Festival. They were going to honor Marianne Drew with a Key to the Village due to her generosity.

"She's right, you know." Darren finally looked up, taking me out of my thoughts on how happy I was for Mama and what she'd done with this building.

No matter how much Darren stuck his head in those books, he surely didn't look the part of a lawyer in his wrinkled shirt with its long sleeves haphazardly rolled up or with his long hair that hung down in the back.

"That doesn't sound very appetizing at all," he said, his dark eyes almost hidden by his thick brows.

He smirked, knowing just how to push Mama's buttons.

"That's right," she agreed. Mama stuck out her tongue and then disappeared.

"You know what's not appetizing?" I glanced across the large community table. The afternoon sun filtered through the skylights, which were original to the old building.

The sunshine was very deceptive. If I were to walk outside of the Leisure Center, the weather would be much different.

Autumn had made what felt like an overnight rush into Holiday Junction.

Darren's comment about Tofurky still hung in the air as the amber light of late afternoon painted everything in warm hues. I couldn't help but gaze out of the Leisure Center's windows, momentarily lost in the beauty of Holiday Junction during this season.

"Holiday Junction is something else during the fall," I mused aloud, picturing the village in my mind.

The streets of our small village were lined with tall oak and maple trees, their leaves transforming into a tapestry of reds, oranges, and golds. It looked as though the mountains themselves caught fire in autumn, their slopes a riot of color, contrasting beautifully with the serene blue of the sea on the other side.

The countryside rolled out in stretches of harvested golden fields, dotted with pumpkins and chrysanthemums. Farmers would set up stands selling fresh apple cider, and children would run around, their laughter echoing as they jumped into heaps of raked leaves. The scent of burning wood would drift from chimneys, mingling with the ever-present aromas of baked goods and roasting nuts.

Local stores had already started their fall displays. Hand-knit scarves in seasonal colors hung in Emily's Treasure's shop window, and Brewing Beans had a sign promising the return of their famous pumpkin spice latte. Even the lampposts were wrapped in strands of orange and yellow fairy lights, creating a soft glow that would soon offset the season's earlier evenings.

"You know," I continued, turning back to Darren with a smile, "as much as Mama huffs and puffs about changes, there's something inherently comforting about the traditions here. The decorations, the food, the colors... It's all butter to the soul."

Darren chuckled, closing his law book for a moment. "Agreed. It's one of the reasons I've never left. Holiday Junction in the fall? There's nothing quite like it."

I nodded. As the *Junction Journal*'s editor in chief, I was fortunate to have a front-row seat to all the village's stories. But it was at times like this, during the embrace of autumn, that I felt a deeper connection.

Here, amidst the cozy traditions and the picturesque setting, was where stories truly came alive. And as the leaves fell, blanketing the village, I couldn't help but feel grateful to be right in the middle of it all.

"I'm really excited about Mama hosting Friendsgiving." I shrugged. "Maybe it'll be in the art district a little closer to the village."

I'd only really discovered the art district a few months ago. It was literally its own community, and from what I gathered and was still investigating, the two communities were always at odds with each other.

After I'd discovered the locals' attitudes, I took a vested interest in covering all the local government meetings as well as the chamber of commerce meetings, since the people there made most of the business decisions about shops and future mercantile endeavors.

Darren shifted from a seat at a corner table while a familiar smell drifted through the room.

The aroma of pumpkin spice from Brewing Beans reached us, and I took a deep breath, savoring the comforting scent.

"I'd only been in Holiday Junction a year, but that scent has quickly become synonymous with autumn," I remarked, thinking of how each year, the scent seemed to weave itself deeper into my memories. "We need to go down and see Hazelynn. She said everything was going fast," I said, talking about Hazelynn Hudson, the owner of and baker at Brewing Beans.

Darren looked over with a smile that was tinged with something else. He inhaled deeply, a look of nostalgia passing over his face.

"It reminds me of when I was a kid," he began, the distant gleam in his eyes showing he was years away. "Every fall, my mom would bring home a fresh-baked pumpkin pie and a steaming cup of pumpkin spice latte. The house would be filled with this aroma for days."

I nodded, appreciating the sentiment, since I could see his mama, Louise Strickland, doing those things for their family. She and Marge Strickland owned the *Junction Journal*. Marge was definitely not the mothering type Louise had been.

Something about this town and its traditions could quickly make anyone feel at home, but for those who grew up here, the connection ran even deeper.

Suddenly, Darren chuckled, drawing me from my musings. "Speaking of traditions, have I ever told you about the Leaf Dance?"

I shook my head, always eager to learn more about the intricacies of Holiday Junction.

"You should've seen it when we were kids," he said, his voice soft with remembrance. "Every year, as the trees began to shed their leaves, the entire town would gather in Holiday Park near the fountain. Kids, adults, everyone would dance and play, kicking up the fallen leaves, laughing and singing. The village would come alive with colors and stories from the elders."

I tried to picture the scene—the square alive with children laughing, elders sharing tales of yore, and the vibrancy of the autumn leaves swirling around the people. It sounded magical.

5

Darren's gaze became distant. "That was the essence of Holiday Junction," he continued. "It wasn't just about the decorations or the food. It was about the community coming together, sharing in the joys and traditions passed down through generations."

"We need to do that." I gasped, looking around to make sure no one was nearby to hear.

"What?" Darren snickered.

"As the you-know-whats," I whispered, my head cocked to the side and down to the ground, so no one would hear me as I discussed our Merry Maker duties with him.

"Oh," he said, smiling with a little glint in his eyes. "That's a great idea. The sign can be life-sized leaves in a dancing pattern." He used hand gestures to show how he envisioned Vern Mckenna was making the wood sign, which Darren and me set up in the wee hours of the morning without anyone seeing us.

"Help! Please, someone help!" Our conversation was shattered by a bloodcurdling scream, unmistakably Mama's.

Darren and I exchanged a glance of alarm before racing out of the dining area, our feet pounding the tile floor. The echoing scream seemed to come from the hall leading to the delivery entrance. We burst from the hallway and into the vicinity of the entrance's staircase, where we found a horrifying sight.

Mama stood there, her face pale, her trembling hands covering her mouth. At her feet lay Albert Harden, the kind man who had delivered milk to Holiday Junction residents for as long as I could remember. His body was crumpled awkwardly at the bottom of the steps leading to the loading dock. From where I stood, it looked like a tragic accident, like he had slipped while descending the steps to his delivery truck.

"Oh, Albert," Mama sobbed, her voice quivering. "I just came out to check on a delivery and... and there he was."

Darren moved quickly to Albert's side, checking for a pulse, while I took Mama into my arms and tried to soothe her racing heart.

"It's going to be okay, Mama," I whispered, though I wasn't sure of that. I took out my phone from my pocket and dialed 911.

"911. What's your emergency?" the operator asked.

Darren looked up, his expression grave. "He's gone, Violet."

A cold shiver ran down my spine.

CHAPTER TWO

L ike everything else in Holiday Junction, it didn't take long for Chief Matthew Strickland, his deputies, and the EMTs to get to the Leisure Center. Nor did it take long for the ambulance chasers to spread the word around town that something sinister had happened.

Darren, Mama, and I sat at the banquet table in the dining hall, waiting to give Matthew our statements. The Leisure Center had become the heart of Holiday Junction's community gathering. The long banquet hall where we sat was adorned with festive decorations that seemed to embody the very essence of this week's Thanksgiving festival.

Mama had used her Southern traditions all over the holidays, and by that, I meant anything Mama had her hand in was decorated to the hilt, every holiday celebration included. Since she owned the Leisure Center, she had a room dedicated to storing all things holiday.

It looked like Thanksgiving had thrown up all over this place.

Tall, freestanding candlesticks, alternating in heights, sat regally on the tables. Their orange and deep-red candles burned softly, lending a warm, flickering glow. Between them lay garlands made of dried autumn leaves, intertwined with cranberries and gold-threaded twine, casting a festive border along each table's length.

On the walls, large wreaths made of twigs formed perfect circles. They held a multitude of decorations: from miniature golden pumpkins and cornucopias filled with faux harvests to delicate feathers that mimicked a turkey's. The wreaths were an ode to nature's bounty, with their plethora of textures and rich autumnal colors ranging from deep plum to burnt orange.

The windowsills weren't left bare either. On each lay small, burlap-wrapped pots, every one holding a single golden sunflower, its head bowed slightly, as if nodding its agreement with the season or winking at Mama.

High above, from the ceiling, hung delicate strands of fairy lights. Their soft golden glow intermingled with the amber hues of the hanging glass lanterns, each painted with scenes of families around dinner tables or children playing amidst fallen leaves. I had no idea where Mama even got things like this, but she did. I wasn't about to question her.

I actually liked it. Reminded me of my childhood and even my adulthood. It didn't matter if it was still ninety degrees outside when the calendar flipped to fall. She had everything in the house decorated in pumpkins, leaves, and scarecrows. The house stopped smelling like summer flowers and started smelling like pumpkin spice lattes. Even the food changed from grilled chicken to hearty soups.

When Mama and Daddy moved to Holiday Junction, she brought the Southern touches with her. I wasn't sure Holiday Junction would ever be the same if something happened to Mama. At first, everyone was a smidgen leery of Mama and her intentions when she did what we liked to call "Southernifying" things. That was when she'd put her special touches on something that took it to a whole other level.

Take this dining hall, for instance. Did the windowsills really need something fallish sitting in them? No, but if you asked her, she'd look at you like you had no sense in even asking such a question. Then she'd bless your heart in a sympathetic way like you'd been missing out on something all your life.

It was Mama's way, and if I had to say so, I'd say she'd brought her own kind of holiday magic to Holiday Junction.

While we waited, I didn't waste any time getting in touch with Radley Jordon, the *Junction Journal*'s newest staff member, to let him know what was going on.

"I need you to find me all the information you can about Albert Harden," I said. Then I began to go down the list of things I would need for an obituary.

They were the things that I didn't like to collect. As the newest employee to hold the title, I took the role of the editor in chief to a new level and had started to delegate tasks in and around the office.

This position had taken me a few months to accept, especially since I was used to being in charge of everything. And I kind of liked it that way.

Marge and Louise Strickland didn't like it that way, which was why Marge had hired Radley without me knowing. He showed up on the front porch of the *Junction Journal*'s seaside office with suitcase in hand, announcing who he was and that he was ready to work.

After a few months, it became apparent that he wouldn't go away no matter what, making me embrace the change and release a little bit of control.

The real issue for me wasn't so much giving him a role at the paper as it was seeing the end of the vision I'd had for it. After all, when I took the job, there was literally nothing that I'd consider an actual newspaper. Rumor was that the Stricklands were going to shut it down, but I'd spent the better part of six months putting in days, nights, and weekends and even dreaming about the *Junction Journal* as I came up with ways to save it.

With Mama and me there, it'd gained some life. Not only did sales of physical copies of the weekly edition of the *Junction Journal* double. We'd even created a subscription to an online daily edition too. That one was thriving.

"Go into the online edition," I instructed him, since I wasn't at the office, and this matter was of the upmost importance. "On the side ticker, it's happening now."

The online paper had a new section, a real-time ticker with current events. Mainly, it was for announcing road closures, reminders of meetings for later in the day, or sightings of missing pets, but not today. Today the ticker was for us to get ahead of whatever telephone gossip would swirl about Mama's Leisure Center.

"You can't do that." Mama touched my hand. When I looked down at it, she wagged her finger.

A heavy silence settled over the dining hall. The waiting felt endless, and every minute ticked by in a slow, torturous fashion. The muffled chatter from down the hall seemed to grow louder, pulling my attention.

"I don't understand what's taking them so long," Mama remarked, her voice thick with anxiety.

Darren's eyes flitted toward the entrance, where his father and the deputies had gone. "You know how thorough Dad can be," he said, though I detected a hint of concern in his eyes.

I squeezed Mama's hand reassuringly. "Maybe we should go see what's going on. The longer this drags out, the more the rumor mill will churn."

Darren nodded. "Right. And knowing this town, by tomorrow there'll be stories about alien abductions and secret underground societies."

As we made our way down the corridor, the seriousness of the situation weighed heavily on me. The usually vibrant and energetic Leisure Center now felt ominous. Even the cute majestic wooden cart filled with pumpkins, gourds, and sheaves of wheat that Mama positioned in the corner of the hallway didn't give me the holiday feels I'd felt when I first passed by it this morning.

We approached the entrance, where Chief Strickland and his team were deep in discussion. As we drew closer, the chief's gaze landed on us.

"Darren, Violet, Millie Kay," Chief Strickland said, his voice somber.

"Matthew, why is this taking so long? The whole town must be talking by now." Mama stepped forward, her voice wavering. Nervously, she wrung her hands.

Mama loved to be the topic of conversation as long as people were saying something good. A dead body wasn't what she'd call good.

Chief Strickland sighed, his eyes filled with a mix of concern and weariness. "It's not as straightforward as it seems, Millie. There's some... discrepancies. We're trying to piece together what happened."

Darren's brow furrowed. "Discrepancies? You mean there's a chance it wasn't an accident?"

Chief Strickland held up his hand. "I don't want to jump to conclusions just yet. But we need to investigate every possibility."

The gravity of that statement settled heavily on our shoulders. Whatever had happened, Holiday Junction was about to experience a Thanksgiving unlike any other.

As the chief moved back to his team, Darren, Mama, and I exchanged worried glances. Whatever was unfolding was bigger than any of us had anticipated.

Darren shuffled Mama back into the hallway, while I stood there waiting to see if I could overhear Matthew talking to Curtis Robinson, the village coroner.

My ears perked when I heard Curtis mention that something about the way Albert fell was suspicious. The way he landed on his back with one leg cocked to the side while the other leg was lying on the first few steps indicated to Curtis that Albert was pushed.

Then there were scraps of drywall underneath Albert's nails like he'd tried to grab for something, which would account for the orange streamers Mama had taped up on the wall that were now ripped and dangling.

I looked along the wall and saw where Curtis had pointed out chunks of missing drywall that were visibly underneath Albert's fingernails.

Matthew glanced up at me and pointed for me to come over to them.

Steeling myself, I walked over to where Chief Strickland stood. The situation grew heavier with each step. His typically friendly gaze was replaced with a serious, investigative look I'd seen in only the most severe circumstances.

"Violet," he started, looking at me intently. "I know this is hard, but I need to ask you some questions. Please, just recount everything from when you first heard the scream."

I nodded, taking a deep breath. As I began retelling the events, I scanned the area. Deputies moved with efficiency, snapping photos of the scene. Their movements had an eerie choreography—each deputy knowing exactly what to do. Some were carefully lifting prints, and others were collecting samples. The coroner, Curtis, was bent over Albert, examining his body meticulously, paying particular attention to his hands and the chunks of drywall lodged under his nails.

"I..." I hesitated, recalling the scream that broke the cozy ambience. "I was in the dining hall with Darren and Mama. We were discussing the upcoming Friendsgiving when we heard Mama scream. We ran out, and that's when we saw... Albert."

Matthew's gaze never wavered. "Did you notice anyone else in the vicinity? Any unfamiliar faces or odd behavior leading up to the incident?"

"No, not that I can recall," I replied. "It was just a regular morning, and then... this."

"And you're sure you didn't see or hear anything unusual before the scream?"

I shook my head. "No. Nothing at all. I was engrossed in our conversation and the decorations. It all happened so suddenly."

Matthew nodded, jotting down a few more notes. "All right. Thank you, Violet. We might need to ask you some more questions later on."

The mechanical clicks of camera shutters punctuated the tense silence. The once joyous Thanksgiving preparation area had transformed into an active crime scene. And all I could do was watch, feeling sadness, shock, and a burning need to uncover what truly happened.

I heard Matthew tell one of the deputies to go get Mama for questioning as I walked past them and down the other set of stairs on the opposite side of the loading dock.

I was immediately met with the view of Albert's familiar delivery truck. It was hard to imagine that just a few hours earlier, he'd been alive and ready for another day's work. I approached the truck cautiously, not wanting to disturb any potential evidence. Though my primary job was that of an editor, my inner investigative journalist was always just beneath the surface.

The back door of the truck was slightly ajar, which was odd. Albert was meticulous about keeping his deliveries in perfect order, a trait everyone in Holiday Junction had come to appreciate.

Peering inside, I was taken aback by the state of disarray. Crates of dairy products were toppled over, milk bottles shattered and their contents pooling on the truck bed's metal surface. Paper invoices and checklists, once neatly clipped to the truck's inside wall, were now strewn about.

It looked like a struggle had taken place inside the truck, or at the very least, like someone had been hastily searching for something. But what could they possibly be looking for in a milk truck?

A feeling of unease settled over me. While I didn't find any direct clues pointing at the attacker, the chaotic state of the truck's interior only added to the mounting evidence that Albert's fall hadn't been accidental. There was more to this matter than met the eye. But what? What had Albert gotten himself into?

Taking one last look, I quickly snapped a couple of photos with my phone for reference then carefully closed the truck door. I made my way back to one of the deputies and pointed out what I'd seen, adding that maybe they should look for evidence in there, before I slipped off and headed around the building.

"Radley, scratch the ticker," I called him, tugging on the edges of my jacket to shield against the cool autumn breeze that was rustling the leaves on the trees.

I could hear the hustle and bustle of the street ahead as I proceeded toward town. The familiar scent of burning wood from fireplaces combined with the earthy aroma of fallen leaves. To my left and right, large ceramic pots filled with vibrant chrysanthemums in shades of burnt orange, deep maroon, and bright yellow lined the sidewalk, forming a stark contrast to the gray of the cobblestone.

The early afternoon sun cast a golden hue, its rays slanting through the nearly bare branches of the trees, leaving dappled patterns on the ground. Every step I took made a gentle crunching sound, the leaves underfoot a testament to the season. Even in the beauty of autumn, though, a heaviness settled in my chest, a mix of grief for Albert and the chilling realization that his death might not have been a mere accident.

Radley's voice came through the phone, his tone concerned. "Violet? What's going on? Why are we scratching the ticker?"

I took a deep breath, trying to steady myself. "Albert's fall... It's looking more and more suspicious. The truck was in a mess, Radley. It feels like there's more to the story, and I don't want to fan the flames of gossip until we know more."

He paused for a moment. "All right, I trust your judgment. We'll hold off on publishing anything until we have a clearer picture."

I sighed, grateful for Radley's understanding. "Thanks, Radley. I'll update you as soon as I have more information."

The conversation ended, and I slipped my phone back into my pocket, gazing at the streets of Holiday Junction. Though the beauty of the season surrounded me, the shadows of doubt and unease had started to creep in. Whatever had happened to Albert, I was determined to find it out.

CHAPTER THREE

D*ing, ding.*

The bell of the trolley clanked as the vehicle made the turn-about in front of Holiday Park, abruptly stopping next to me.

"Where you goin'?" Goldie Bennett asked after she flung the trolley door open. Dressed in her usual seasonal flair, she had dangling turkey earrings that moved with every turn of her head and a light-up necklace adorned with colorful plastic fall leaves illuminating her throat.

"The office." I pointed past the Holiday Park Fountain and toward the path that led down to the shoreline where the office was located.

Everything in Holiday Junction was so close that trying to drive somewhere was ridiculous because it would take longer to park than to hoof it. Feet, golf carts, and bicycles were the preferred modes of transportation. Since I needed to think, I'd decided to walk instead of bike.

Goldie leaned a bit farther out, her brows raised inquisitively, the light of curiosity burning in her eyes.

"What's all that ruckus going on at the Leisure Center?" she asked, knowing I'd have the information.

I hesitated for a moment, trying to figure how much to share, but with Goldie, it was always better to be forthcoming; she'd find out anyway.

"Albert Harden was found at the bottom of the stairs. Chief Strickland and Curtis believe it might be foul play," I said.

Goldie's face turned ashen.

"Albert? But..." Her voice trailed off, the impact of the news evident.

"Yes, and word's spreading fast." I glanced around and saw people huddled together, no doubt discussing the news as they all looked at me, knowing I was Mama's daughter.

Goldie looked away, processing what I'd shared.

"You know, I saw a group of women speed-walking toward Peppermint Court like their pants were on fire when I was parked at the stop down there. Overheard one of them whispering about the Leisure Center and Albert. Seems everyone's heading to the Hardens' residence to rubberneck," she said, her lips twitching.

That didn't surprise me. In a tight-knit community like Holiday Junction, news traveled faster than wildfire, especially aboard Goldie's trolley. I frowned, thinking about the added grief the knowledge of Albert's death would cause his wife.

"I need to get to the Hardens' before the gossip mill goes into overdrive," I said, hoping to get some leads on why someone would want to hurt Albert or even just go through his delivery truck.

Goldie nodded, her face solemn. "Hop on, I'll get you there in no time."

As I climbed aboard, Goldie's demeanor softened.

"Albert's wife... She and I were like two peas in a pod, you know? After their boy..." She trailed off, her voice thick with emotion.

"Really?" I said gently, placing a reassuring hand on Goldie's arm, not asking a question as much as being shocked by the sad news about Albert's past. "I had no idea. I met him a few times when he was delivering at the Leisure Center. Mama doesn't need a lot of milk there each week, but this week she had a big order because she's hosting the village's Friendsgiving on Wednesday night."

I took my seat behind Goldie and grabbed the handle that dangled near my head.

She pulled the handle in, slamming the trolley door shut.

The trolley took off, and we made our way toward Peppermint Court.

The vehicle chugged into motion down Main Street. The sidewalks were filled with tourists and folks in town specifically for the Thanksgiving holiday. After all, holidays were what we based our tourist marketing on, and we were good at it.

Brewing Beans was at its peak hour. Patrons were sitting outside, the soft haze of their warm breath mixing with the aroma of fresh brew. Every morning before work, I made sure to stop in and see Hazelynn for a fresh cup of coffee to get me started.

"We used to meet up at Emily's Treasures," Goldie reminisced, her voice tinged with nostalgia as we passed the boutique. "Tara loved to hunt for jewelry there. She had an eye for fashion."

The trolley rolled past Flowerworks Florist, where a dazzling display of autumn bouquets stood out front, their fiery hues mirroring the vibrant colors of the trees lining the streets. Betsy Carmichael had the cutest flower shop display I'd ever seen.

Flowerworks Florist was nothing short of enchanting. Betsy Carmichael, with her meticulous attention to detail, had transformed the storefront into an intimate autumnal haven. Rustic wooden barrels were positioned at intervals, each brimming with bunches of marigolds, chrysanthemums, and asters. Their warm shades of orange, gold, and deep burgundy spilled over, creating cascades of color that led visitors to the entrance.

Beside the barrels, tall wrought iron stands draped with ivy showcased vases bearing more exotic blooms, their fragrant scent wafting in the breeze. Overhead, a wooden archway, wrapped in twinkling fairy lights, beckoned visitors beneath it. From the archway hung delicate glass jars, inside of which single blossoms floated in water, catching the sunlight in the most ethereal way.

But what truly made Flowerworks stand apart was the sensory experience Betsy curated. As you approached, the soft melodies of wind chimes blended with the aromas of fresh earth and blooms, creating an almost magical aura. Entering Flowerworks felt less like walking into a shop and more like stepping into an ever-evolving floral symphony, orchestrated by Betsy's passion for her craft.

My heart fluttered with anticipation as we passed by the Jubilee Inn. It was the first place I had stayed when I moved to Holiday Junction. Kristine and Hurbert Whitlock made it so nice to live there, even though I was taking up a room for other guests.

The inn's welcoming lights were prepped for the evening guests who were there to have the Thanksgiving meet and greet with the village mayor—Mayor Paisley.

Mayor Paisley wasn't just any old mayor. Our mayor was a Boston terrier. Mm-hmmm, a dog.

A cute dog that had won the election against other furry citizens and was voted on by the good folks of Holiday Junction. The village was really run by the town council, and the mayoral election cost a dollar to vote in on top of the cost to have a photo opportunity with Mayor Paisley, but all the proceeds went back into Holiday Junction's marketing.

The photo opportunities were cute, and when they could, visitors came from far and wide to get a photo with her.

A lunch line had formed outside of Freedom Diner. The restaurant's neon sign, reading Open, cast a soft glow.

Goldie continued, taking me out of my thoughts, "When their boy passed, Tara and I would meet at the diner, you know? It was our safe space, a place to share, cry, and remember."

As the downtown gave way, the landscape started to shift. Old mansions with large hedged fences hinted at Holiday Junction's richer history. Before too long, we'd passed the Strickland compound, where the whole family lived except for Darren and his cousin Rhett.

Then the road gently curved, revealing sprawling fields adorned with golden sunflowers standing tall, their heads tilted toward the sun as we headed out past the village countryside.

"And every autumn," Goldie went on, her tone softening as she recalled her history at every single turn, "we'd pick sunflowers together. She said they reminded her of hope in darker times."

As we neared the seaside, the fall winds picked up, carrying with them the salty tang of the ocean. High above, colorful kites danced, their tails fluttering like flags of joy against the azure sky. During the fall, that was a common sight.

Finally, the trolley took a right down Peppermint Court.

"Tara was more than just a friend, Violet. She was family. And today, I fear what this news will do to her," Goldie sighed.

"You don't think she already knows?" I asked when we passed by a group of women carrying food dishes in their arms.

The Harden residence, nestled at the heart of Peppermint Court, was a quintessential representation of autumn's embrace. The front yard boasted a beautifully curated landscape where rows of marigold, aster, and chrysanthemums flourished, encircled by a picket fence draped with garlands of red and gold leaves, intertwined with twinkling fairy lights. A cluster of hay bales was neatly stacked near the entrance, and close by sat carved pumpkins, their faces lit with soft, warm candles, giving the yard a magical glow.

Sitting atop one hay bale was a decorative scarecrow in a plaid shirt and overalls, its straw hat tilted just so, as if it were tipping its hat to everyone who passed by. A wooden sign stood beside it, reading, "Give thanks. Celebrate love." Swirls of colorful leaves had been painted onto the path leading up to the Hardens' front door, guiding visitors on a festive journey.

As I took in the serene autumn beauty of the Harden home, Goldie's voice pulled me back to the drama unfolding on the street.

"Look there," she spat with venom, pointing to a tall, slender woman with raven-black hair. "Who does Clarissa think she is? She and Tara never got along. Just look at her with that casserole dish. She's only going to nose around!"

Without waiting for me, Goldie charged forward like a bull, her face red and indignant.

"You stop right there, Clarissa!" she ordered, holding out her hand authoritatively, reminiscent of Mrs. Bailey, the crossing guard at the local elementary school. "I dare you to step another foot into that yard!"

Clarissa, momentarily caught off guard, looked from the casserole dish in her hand to Goldie's furious face, her own expression a mix of surprise and defiance.

Clarissa put her hand on her hip, and the casserole dish teetered in one hand.

While the two of them hashed it out with all eyes on them, I took the dish from Clarissa. She gave me a thankful look when I got the opposite from Goldie.

Then Clarissa and Goldie started pointing at each other, wagging fingers and making all sorts of claims about one another as I slipped past them, casserole in hand, going around the house to see if I could notice Tara inside.

"Hello?" I called into the screen door from the porch. "Mrs. Harden?" I asked before I saw the kitchen table set for lunch or what looked like a luncheon of sorts.

There were tiered dishes with finger sandwiches and some little petits fours. Some sort of luncheon was definitely meant to happen here.

"Mrs. Harden?" I called again, taking a step closer to the door. "It's Violet Rhinehammer."

I balanced the dish on a flat palm and covered my brow with my free hand, taking a closer look through the screen door and into the house.

My gaze traveled down to the kitchen floor.

Tara Harden lay there, her head tilted toward the door, eyes open. Dead.

CHAPTER FOUR

T he afternoon sun cast eerie shadows across Tara Harden's quaint kitchen. The once inviting space now felt cold and foreign, tainted by an unspeakable tragedy. I swallowed the lump forming in my throat as the situation pressed heavily on my chest. It was unfathomable—two deaths in the same family within mere hours.

Chief Strickland moved about carefully, ensuring he didn't disturb any potential evidence. His deep-set eyes scoured every inch of the scene, pausing momentarily on Mrs. Harden's still form before continuing with the meticulous attention of a seasoned detective.

"I can't believe we're standing in another crime scene," I whispered more to myself than to anyone around.

Strickland's gaze found mine, reflecting my own shock and disbelief.

"Rhinehammer," he said, breaking the silence between us. "I know this might sound unconventional, but we need your help."

I raised an eyebrow, my curiosity piqued.

"Our photographer is still tied up at the Leisure Center," he explained. "We need photographs of this scene before we can move Mrs. Harden."

I nodded and took out my phone. "Of course, Chief. Whatever you need."

As I began taking photos, my journalistic instincts kicked into high gear. The shots I took were not just for evidence but for a story, one the people of this town deserved to know. The overturned furniture, the shattered pieces of porcelain scattered across the floor, the stark contrast of Tara's pale, lifeless face against the vibrant fall decor of her home—they all told a tale of chaos and desperation.

After snapping a series of photos, I noticed a drawer slightly ajar with papers strewn about inside. Could the intruder have been looking for something specific? What was so important that it drove them to commit such heinous acts?

The room buzzed with an electric tension, the presence of unsolved mysteries thickening the very air around us with anticipation. Murmurs began to ripple through the crowd gathering outside the Harden residence. Word traveled fast in small towns, and the twin tragedies had already become the talk of the hour.

I approached Chief Strickland, showing him the photos I had taken. "Looks like they were searching for something," I said, pointing at the disheveled drawer.

He nodded. "Yes, and whatever it is, they're desperate enough to kill for it. We need to find out what it is—and fast."

"Does that mean you're looking into their deaths as a homicide?" I asked, since I'd yet to hear this tidbit of news.

"I didn't say that," Matthew Strickland snapped back, as though he didn't mean to let those thoughts slip past his mouth.

"Right." I nodded. "You mean just because the delivery truck was obviously torn apart by someone looking for something, Albert's death, and now this. I see that there looks like a correlation. I can see why you'd think this was a double homicide with both the Hardens dead. But you're right. I mean, you know, I've heard of couples dying on the same day hours apart because of broken hearts and all that."

I knew there was no way these deaths were accidents. Both husband

and wife dead, both places that were all torn up as if they held deeply buried secrets.

What I did know was Matthew Strickland's ego was of giant proportions, and if I'd kept pressing him on what he let slip by his mouth, he'd kick me out of here and wait however long he had to for the deputy who usually took the photos and bagged a lot of the evidence.

"I'll go take some more photos," I said and pointed up the stairs just off the kitchen while he looked over more of the items dumped on the floor near Tara's body.

I made my way up the creaky stairs, trying to move silently, though I wasn't sure why. I supposed I just didn't want to disturb anything. Every step I took was like walking through an autumn wonderland. The Hardens had clearly loved this time of year. Garlands of rich golden and deep-red leaves draped the stairway railings. On the landing, a welcome mat rested under my feet with the cheerful proclamation "Happy fall, y'all."

More fall decorations adorned the hallway. Lanterns filled with tiny LED fairy lights and surrounded by an assortment of pumpkins were placed along its length. Painted wooden signs leaned against the walls, with phrases like "Fall is my favorite color" and "Harvest blessings."

I entered what seemed to be a home office or a study. The first thing that caught my eye was a beautifully decorated desk calendar.

Curious, I moved closer. A list of names was scribbled on the square for today's date, and they were all for a brunch Tara had planned. My eyes scanned through the unfamiliar names until one caught my attention—Betsy Carmichael. I knew her. She was the charming lady who owned Flowerworks Florist.

The realization made me even more anxious. If Betsy was meant to be here for brunch, did she know about the tragedy? I pulled out my phone and captured a quick shot of the calendar. It was a long shot, but perhaps these women had answers, or at the very least, Betsy might.

I needed to tread carefully. This scenario wasn't just a story; it was the lives of people in my community, and I needed to respect that. I took one last look around the room and made mental notes of any other potential clues before I headed back downstairs.

As I descended the stairs, my shoes gently tapping against the wooden steps, I saw Matthew rise from his hunched position by Tara's body. Curtis Robinson, the town's lanky coroner, had joined him. He was taking a preliminary look at Tara's lifeless form, his brows furrowed in concentration.

Matthew's gaze met mine as I approached. He had a mix of curiosity and impatience in his eyes.

"Violet," he began, his voice measured, "did you find anything... out of place upstairs?"

I took a moment to gather my thoughts.

"Not particularly," I began. "The upstairs seemed... normal. Organized, even. Nothing like the state of this kitchen. It's strange." I gestured to the room around us, the drawers emptied and contents strewn about. "Why cause such havoc here and not elsewhere?"

Without looking up from his work, Curtis chimed in, "Perhaps the search was interrupted? Or maybe they found what they were looking for?"

Matthew's jaw tightened. "Or they knew exactly where to look," he murmured, more to himself than to us.

I met his eyes.

"Which means they might have known Tara personally or were familiar with the house," I suggested. "It's just a hunch." I shrugged, trying to be casual without stating the obvious and appearing as though I was a deputy or the lead detective, which I definitely knew I could do.

Matthew nodded slowly.

"Everything's on the table at this point. But if you're right, it complicates things even more," he said.

Curtis cleared his throat, drawing Matthew's attention and mine.

"From my initial assessment," Curtis began cautiously, "it seems she may have suffered a sudden cardiac event. But of course, an autopsy will provide a clearer picture."

"So it's possible that her death was natural?" I blinked in surprise.

Curtis shrugged slightly.

"Possible but not conclusive. The scene here raises questions. Until I complete the autopsy, everything's speculative."

The room fell silent, the gravity of the situation pressing down on us. Two deaths, a ransacked house, and more questions than answers. This mystery was only deepening, and nothing at this point made sense.

CHAPTER FIVE

I stepped out into the crisp fall air, leaving the disarray of the Harden home behind me yet still feeling that pressure on my chest. After pulling out my phone, I speed-dialed Mama.

Before I could even hear the first ring, movement caught my attention.

Betsy Carmichael, the owner of Flowerworks and one of the names written on Tara's calendar, stood a few feet away, clutching a stunning floral arrangement—a mix of burnt oranges, deep reds, and golden yellows, evoking the very essence of fall.

Our eyes met briefly. I could discern a myriad of emotions: shock, fear, and something else I couldn't quite place. Before I could say anything, Betsy's face paled, and she looked away.

Without uttering a word, she hurriedly walked over to her parked golf cart and placed the arrangement on the passenger seat. With a swift motion, she took off, the wheels of the cart crunching over the fall leaves littering the road.

"Strange," I muttered to myself. The phone in my hand buzzed, indicating Mama was on the line, but I was momentarily lost in thought, wondering why Betsy made such a hasty exit.

"Violet? Honey, is that you?" Mama's voice pulled me back to the present.

"Yeah, Mama, it's me. Just wanted to check in on you. Are you okay?" I asked, not yet telling her about Tara.

Before I could hear her reply, a voice called out from the house next door to the Harden residence. "Hey, Violet!"

I squinted against the afternoon sun, recognizing Mrs. Penelope Caldwell, a petite woman in her sixties, waving at me from her porch, a curious look in her eyes.

"I've got to go, Mama. Mrs. Caldwell is calling me over. I'll call you back," I told Mama.

"Penelope Caldwell?" Mama asked. "Why on earth—" She abruptly stopped talking as though she knew. "Violet Rhinehammer, are you over there bugging Tara for a story?"

"Not at all, Mama." I sighed and waved back at Mrs. Caldwell. "She is the story," I said and quickly gave Mama a rundown about what had happened.

"Well, you get on over to Penelope's and see what she's got to say, that meddlin' old coot." Mama would never say that in front of anyone but me.

Penelope Caldwell, the Hardens' next-door neighbor, had always been a fountain of information. With her house perfectly positioned to oversee most of the comings and goings on Peppermint Court, she had an uncanny ability to know almost everything that happened in the neighborhood.

She was always calling the *Junction Journal* hotline with gossip to put in the paper's society pages. Most of it was nosy and didn't make the news, but today, matters just might have been different.

I walked over to the white picket fence separating the two properties, offering a half smile. "Mrs. Caldwell," I said to her, "how are you today?"

"Oh, Violet, dear, never mind that. What on earth happened next door? It's been a flurry of activity all morning!" Her voice was filled with a mix of genuine concern and unabashed curiosity, a classic trait of small-town life.

I hesitated, choosing my words carefully.

"It's a bit complicated, Mrs. Caldwell. I promise, once things are clearer, you'll know. For now, it might be best to give the Harden house some space," I said, not wanting to mention any details that would give Matthew a clue that I'd told someone something I shouldn't.

She sighed dramatically, pouting like a child denied candy. "Very well. But you'll tell me if you hear anything?"

I nodded, suppressing a smile. "Of course, Mrs. Caldwell." Then I sensed an opportunity.

"Actually, Mrs. Caldwell," I started, walking around the fence line and meeting her at her porch, "what do you mean there was a flurry of activity this morning?" I tried really hard to walk away. I did. But curiosity got the best of me.

I blamed that on my inner journalist.

She looked away for a moment, scanning the horizon as if digging deeply into her memory. But by the way she looked at me from the corner of her eyes, she was itching to tell me something.

"Well, since you ask, there was a little... incident this morning. Someone from the art district came down. They were having quite the animated discussion with Albert. I wasn't intentionally listening, mind you, but they weren't exactly keeping their voices down."

Intrigued, I raised an eyebrow.

"Do you remember what they looked like? Or maybe what they were arguing about?"

Penelope pursed her lips, her forehead creasing in thought.

"Tall, lanky fellow. Wearing one of those fancy hats... a beret, I think. And a scarf, even though it's not that cold. Typical artiste attire if you ask me. As for the topic, they were going on about some kind of 'agreement' and 'promises.' Albert seemed upset, but the other man, he was downright angry." She didn't give a whole lot to go on, but it was a start.

I nodded, filing away this information.

Villagers had whispered about conflicts between the new residents and the old-timers. But nothing concrete had ever surfaced.

"Thank you, Mrs. Caldwell. That's quite helpful," I said.

"I just hope everything gets sorted out soon." Her voice carried genuine concern. She gave me a wistful smile.

"I hope so too," I replied softly, making a mental note to dig deeper into the goings-on in the art district. The morning's altercation was too significant to ignore. If the artists had any quarrel with Albert, I needed to find out.

"By the way," she called out from the porch, "if you want to know more about the goings-on around the shops and districts you live in, you should probably come to the chamber of commerce meetings and not that feller who runs the paper now."

"He doesn't run the paper," I quickly retorted. "He just works for me."

"Oh, word around town is that he runs it." She tapped her chin. "Or did he say that at the chamber meeting?"

Mrs. Caldwell's words laid down on me, causing my pace to quicken as I took the familiar path down Peppermint Court. How dare Radley? The audacity he had to misrepresent his role at the paper, especially in front of the chamber of commerce.

I tried to shake the frustration, focusing instead on the calming rhythm of the ocean—using the zen stuff they tell you to use, you know, taking and holding deep breaths and all the rest.

Over the last few years, I'd tried to get better at those things. Not jumping the gun, slowing down, but it was hard. My personality didn't agree with all of those things, and when the mind said you gotta just take a deep breath, my personality said, "Go, go, go."

Right now, I was listening to my personality.

CHAPTER SIX

The sea had a different hue than in the hotter months. Instead of the usual deep azure, the waters had become a cooler shade of steel blue, mirroring the overcast sky above. Waves lapped lazily against the shore as if they, too, were trying to savor the last warmth before winter's chill set in.

The salty aroma was also different in the fall. It carried a crispness, mixed with the faint tang of seaweed and the distant scent of wood smoke from fireplaces that had begun to warm the nearby homes.

Seagulls cried out overhead, their calls more plaintive than before, echoing the seasonal shift. A few brave souls wandered the shoreline, wrapped in thick sweaters and scarves, their faces upturned to capture the waning warmth of the sun.

As I approached the dunes, the marram grass appeared more golden than green, swaying gently in the breeze and rustling softly. The sound always reminded me of whispered secrets. I closed my eyes for a moment, letting the symphony of the sea wash over me, grounding me. Trying that zen thing.

I leaned my arm on top of the old white rusty mailbox. The white-painted post had been concreted into the ground. Louise Strickland had taken some of those one-inch-by-two-inch peel-and-stick letters and formed the name *Junction Journal* down the mailbox's side instead of an address.

"Deep breath in," I muttered, letting the sounds of the ocean's eternal ebb and flow become the background noise.

"What are you doing out there?" Radley yelled from the front porch of the *Junction Journal* office, which was really a seaside cottage owned by Rhett Strickland.

The office used to be in the Strickland mansion off Main Street, but when they offered me the job and I took it, I knew I couldn't work in anyone's house if I was going to revitalize the paper.

On a wing, a prayer, and a lot of confidence, I brought the *Junction Journal* back. Now we were operating in the black instead of on life support.

"I'm trying to calm myself down," I muttered underneath a half grin and wave. "I'm coming. Just looking at the kites."

Lie, lie, lie.

I pushed off the mailbox and headed into the office.

"What did you hear?" he asked.

"I need you to pull every chamber of commerce meeting agenda you've attended." I took off my jacket and hung it on the coatrack just inside the door.

Mama also worked, to use the term loosely, at the *Journal* when I needed her to. She was pretty good at finding out information on the internet and going down rabbit holes when I didn't have time to do it.

The cottage was not really in great shape when we first took it over, and I was pleasantly surprised when Rhett agreed to remodel it. We only needed basic things done to get it up and running.

They included things like making sure the roof was solid and the electric was up to date and inspected. The building had a full kitchen, so we only needed a refrigerator and microwave along with the two working bathrooms.

My office was the room off the right from the hallway, and Mama's was on the left, which had become Radley's office over the last few months because Mama had been spending all of her time at the Leisure Center.

Radley looked at me with a furrowed brow, clearly a little taken aback by my sudden urgency.

"All right, all right, give me a second." He headed into his office and started rummaging through his desk, looking for the documents I'd asked for.

I glanced around the room and took in the little office. I loved it despite its previous state. It had character, and the remodeling gave it just the right balance of modern convenience and rustic charm. The wooden beams on the ceiling, the vintage windowpanes, and the creaky floorboards were a testament to the office's history.

After a few moments, Radley pulled out a stack of papers.

"Here's what I have. The last few meetings' agendas," he said and stacked them on the desk.

I took the first one off the top and started to skim through it.

While I did so, he filled me in on that particular chamber of commerce meeting.

"There was this guy from the art district who showed up. Quite persistent. He wanted Albert to start delivering up their way. Claimed they needed fresh products for some of their projects, especially with the art scene booming up there." He looked up from underneath his brows at me.

"And?" I prompted.

"And Albert declined. Politely but firmly. Said his route was full and that he was the only driver. He also mentioned something about sticking to delivering products for the Hippity Hoppity Ranch Farm, since they were the bulk of his business."

"Hippity Hoppity Ranch Farm?" I, too, looked up, thinking that it had been a while since I'd been there and visited with Millard and Tito Ramsey, the mother-and-son duo.

"Yeah," Radley continued. "Did a quick search online after you told me about what happened at the Leisure Center. Turns out Albert was primarily employed by Hippity Hoppity Ranch. They supply a range of organic products. Quite the favorite in town and of neighboring communities."

I took a deep breath. I hated to admit it, but I'd gone there only for the horses. They provided horse rides on the beach for tourists. When I went there, my blinders led me to the ranch part and blocked off the rest of it.

"And this person from the art district—do you remember his name?" I asked and pulled my phone out of my pocket to text Mama.

She must have made contact with Millard Ramsey if she was getting deliveries from Albert.

Radley frowned, trying to recollect.

"I think it was something like... I can check the minutes. They should have it recorded." He turned back to the drawer where he kept the files and started to thumb through them.

"Please do. We need to have a list of potential leads to follow. Even if the police aren't calling this a homicide, there are too many connections here for it to be mere coincidence," I said, determination growing within me. We had a lead, and I intended to follow it to its end. "I'll go start writing it down on our board."

I took the stack of files to my office. My computer buzzed when I placed the files next to its mouse.

Radley had recently gotten another whiteboard. He had made the great suggestion that one board list the events scheduled for the Thanksgiving Festival and another show deadlines and headlines—or at least headline ideas—for the physical paper.

Eager to start fresh, I swiped away old headlines with the eraser. The board gleamed blank and bright under the overhead light. I took a thick black marker, popped off the lid, and wrote "Albert & Tara Harden" in the middle.

Directly below, I wrote "Suspects:," followed by a list. A question mark indicating the unknown name of the man from the art district who Albert had argued with was the first entry. My hand hovered for a moment before I added a tentative question mark. Then I wrote, "Betsy Carmichael." Seeing her name made my stomach hurt.

My fingers instinctively reached for my phone, and I pulled up the photo of Tara's calendar. The dates, names, and notes were all clearly captured. I zoomed in, trying to find any other clue, and then, a tap on the door pulled me from my thoughts.

Radley leaned against the doorframe, a curious expression on his face.

"Got a game plan going?" he asked.

I pointed at the board, specifically at Betsy's name.

"She acted... off earlier, outside the Harden house. I caught her just standing there with a floral arrangement in hand. We made brief eye contact, but she hurried off. Didn't say a word," I said.

Radley's brow furrowed.

"Betsy? The Betsy from Flowerworks Florist? That's... unexpected," he noted. He knew Betsy was a talker. I'd sent him to Flowerworks after he started dating Amelia Hartman to grab her some fresh flowers.

"Right? And there's more." I showed him the photo of Tara's calendar. "She had an upcoming brunch date with Tara. See, right there." I pointed at a date circled in red with "Brunch - Betsy Carmichael" scribbled neatly beside it. "And the table was set for a brunch today."

Radley adjusted his glasses, studying the image.

"You think Betsy had something to do with this?" he asked.

"I don't know yet," I replied, tapping the board. "But her behavior, the brunch... It all connects somehow. We just need to find out how."

He nodded slowly, taking everything in.

"It's a start, at least. If she was scheduled to meet Tara and then appeared at the house acting suspiciously after the incident..." He trailed off, leaving the implication hanging in the air.

"I need to look up the rest of these ladies on the list too." I started writing down their names.

"And there's the whole chamber of commerce angle. Everything is so... intertwined." I sighed, resting my forehead on my hand.

With a steadying breath, I continued to list the names, repeating each one softly as I penned it on the board.

"Daphne Marsh," I muttered, writing it down. "Next is Marianne Drew," I continued. "Cassidy North," I added finally, recognizing her name.

Cassidy was a relatively new face in town. She had quickly made a name for herself as an ambitious real estate agent, always looking for the next big property deal.

She'd actually come into the office to try to purchase it.

I leaned back, observing the growing web of names.

"I only know one of them," I said, circling Cassidy's name. "You remember her, right?"

Radley shook his head.

"She's the one who came in here wanting to purchase the office and said it was a gazillion-dollar property," I exaggerated.

"Oh yeah." Radley nodded. "She even told me if I was interested in looking at something to purchase, she'd be more than happy to help me."

"I'm thinking you are looking for something about now," I said, slowly nodding, giving him the unspoken suggestion that he needed to get in front of her.

"Yeah. I just might be." He grinned and then looked at the weekly events board.

I turned my attention from the suspects board to the weekly events board. Despite the investigation on my mind, the paper had to continue. The events on the second board were colorful and varied, reminding me of the spirit of the town.

"We've got the Pumpkin Patch Visit," I said.

According to the write-up sent in by the Hippity Hoppity Ranch Farm, families would be heading there to pick out the perfect pumpkin.

"The Autumn Art Festival is at the Ceramic Celebration, where artists are going to showcase their work—everything from intricate hand-blown glass to watercolor paintings," I read the description. "Crafting Workshop for kids, where they'd learn to make fall-themed crafts and decorations are also going to be at the Ceramic Celebration."

I moved on down the line.

"Cider Tasting at Cup of Cheer." I was talking about the town tea shop that was going to introduce its new seasonal flavors, from crisp apple to spiced cranberry.

"Sunset Beach Bonfire is at the beach near the lighthouse." I couldn't help but smile when I thought of the lighthouse, since Darren lived there.

"The hayride-and-ghost-stories follow-up at Holiday Park," Radley said in a way that made me think he really wanted to do that.

I glanced his way, which interrupted him.

"I told Amelia I'd like to take her to that." His face reddened like the color of Amelia's hair at the mere thought of her.

"Oh, are you going to pick her up?" I asked.

"I haven't made many plans, but..." His sentence lingered, as though he was waiting for me to respond.

"The Cook-Off Contest is taking place in the art district, and if you're picking her up, maybe you two can cover that for us?" I asked. "I don't think we can count on Mama to do anything today."

I hadn't talked to Mama, but I knew her, and she'd probably taken to the bed now that Albert had died in her presence.

"All right, Radley," I began, glancing between the list and my determined colleague, "I think I'll head over to the Pumpkin Patch and maybe the bonfire later tonight. It might be a good place to overhear things or chat informally. Plus, I love the nostalgia of it all."

He smirked. "You just want a pumpkin spice latte."

"As for you, the Art Festival could be key, especially with our art district lead. And considering Cassidy's profession, you might stumble upon her at the Cook-Off. She might have properties to showcase or want to engage with potential clients. Sounds good?" I asked.

"You want me to charm some information from her?" he asked with a wink.

"Use that Radley charm," I teased. "But seriously, keep it subtle."

I stepped back and looked at the event board and then at what had turned into the murder board, if a murder was involved.

"All right, it's a plan, then. We cover these events but always keep an ear out. You never know where a lead might pop up." I wrote our names next to the events each one of us would be covering.

He nodded, ready to tackle the day's challenges both for the paper and our budding investigation.

CHAPTER SEVEN

The first stop on my way out the door was to the jiggle joint. Though the name didn't create a great image in your mind, it was exactly one of those bars.

Fortunately for me, there wasn't too much jigglin' on stage during the daytime hours here in Holiday Junction, but there was still a lot of bar sittin' and drinkin'.

"Just who I wanted to see," I said as I bellied up to the bar and stood behind Owen and Shawn, the regular barflies. I draped an arm around each one of them. "Happy Thanksgiving week, Easter Bunny," I said directly to Owen, who loved to introduce himself as such. "And you, too, Tooth Fairy." My gaze shifted to Shawn.

"What do you want?" Shawn asked with a look of wonder in his eye.

"Can I get another round here for my friends?" I asked the bartender when she walked up to see what I wanted. "I'll have a Diet Coke."

"She must really need a favor," Owen said, nudging Shawn before sticking up two fingers. "We'll take two rounds."

"Fine," I snickered and then said, "Put it on the Junction Journal tab."

Even though I said to put it on the newspaper's tab, I knew it wouldn't be billed. The jiggle joint was owned by Darren Strickland, who used to be in here all the time, but now that he'd decided to get that law degree, the only place I could find him during the day was at Diffy Delk's office, where he clerked while going to school.

"You two have lived here all your life, and I need some information about a few people." I pulled out my list. "Daphne Marsh and Marianne Drew."

"What do you want to know?" Shawn asked, circling his finger around the lip of his beer mug, creating lines in the condensation.

"Who are they? What do they do? Why would Tara Harden want to have them for a luncheon?" I asked.

"I heard about Albert." Owen grimaced, his lips stretched across his face. "And at the Leisure Center." He tsked. "You never know when it's going to strike."

"Death?" I asked.

"Heart attack." Owen shook his head and picked up his stein then wetted his whistle.

"Heart attack?" I questioned. "Where did you hear that?"

They obviously had not been privy to the fact that I was there, too, and I kept it that way.

"I was down at Doc Pickering's right before lunch to get a refill on my blood pressure meds, and that's when Curtis Robinson came in to get Albert's medical records. Then Doc came back in and said Albert was working his delivery route when he must've had a heart attack." Owen sighed.

"Cheers to Albert," Shawn said. The two lifted their glasses, and I raised my Diet Coke in the air. We tapped them together.

"Unless," Shawn continued as he eyeballed me, "you know something we don't." He cocked a brow.

"Yeah. I mean, you are asking about two very influential women in our village," Owen said.

His words caught my attention.

He gripped his mug handle and took a drink.

"Influential?" I asked.

I had to admit that there were a lot of people I didn't know, and I was still learning my own way around Holiday Junction, so I would gladly take any and all information I could get.

"You tell us." Shawn sat up straight and crossed his arms, waiting for me to say something.

"Tara Harden is dead," I said.

Owen's hand went limp. The mug tumbled out of his grip.

"Oh man," Owen cried out as the beer puddled on top of the bar then spilled all over his pants. "I've wasted my beer."

"Dead?" Shawn asked, uncurling his arms.

The force of my words hung in the air for a moment, with Owen mourning his beer and Shawn slowly processing the news.

Owen finally looked up, his earlier jovial demeanor gone.

"Tara Harden... dead?" His voice was thick with emotion.

Shawn, always the more perceptive of the two despite his laid-back appearance, narrowed his eyes at me.

"You think there's foul play?" he asked.

I took a deep breath. "It's just... all the evidence doesn't add up to a simple heart attack or a natural death for Tara. Especially not after what happened at the Leisure Center."

Owen, having composed himself, signaled the bartender for another beer.

"So you think these women are connected?" Owen asked.

"It's possible," I admitted. "But I need to know more about them to make any connections. I had gone over to her house, and that's when I..."

"You found her?" Owen's eyes grew big.

I nodded.

"The kitchen table was set for a luncheon. On her calendar were the women's names," I said, leaving out Betsy Carmichael. "They didn't show up while I was there, to my knowledge, and this all does look very suspicious, which makes me wonder if there was foul play."

"How did Tara die?" Shawn asked.

"I don't know." I shrugged. "I didn't see anything visible."

Shawn leaned back, taking a moment before speaking. "Well,

Daphne Marsh—she's old money here in Holiday Junction. Family's been in the town for generations. They used to own most of the farmlands around here before selling them off. She's got her hands in a lot of businesses, real estate mostly, but she also sits on several charity boards. Always looking for a good PR opportunity. She does own the Festive Finds Thrift Store. Mainly just to bide time, from what I understand."

I jotted that down mentally. Daphne Marsh—old money, business, real estate, Festive Finds.

"And Marianne Drew?" I prompted.

Owen took the lead this time. "She's a different story. Not from here originally but has been around for a good twenty years or so. Runs the most successful charity gala every year, the Mistletoe Masquerade Charity Ball. Everyone who's anyone in town attends. Raises a ton of money for different causes. But word is, she's a bit of a control freak. Wants to oversee everything and make all the decisions and doesn't like being told no."

"Sounds like a fun time," I remarked, thinking of how two highly influential women might have crossed paths with Tara.

"Well, if you're looking for a connection," Shawn began. Then he paused and sipped his beer. "Daphne has been wanting to develop the land next to the Leisure Center for years. She's proposed a few luxury condos but has always been shot down because of zoning laws and a lot of community pushback. Tara was a vocal critic. And Marianne? She's been trying to get the community to have the ball up in the art district as the new venue for her annual ball for the past two years. Tara was on the committee that kept rejecting her proposal. Said it wasn't 'exclusive' enough."

I frowned, digesting his words.

"So both women had disagreements with Tara. Public disagreements," I noted.

"Looks that way," Owen confirmed, rubbing the back of his neck.

Shawn gave me a sidelong glance. "You're going down a rabbit hole here, Violet. These are big names in Holiday Junction. If you start pointing fingers, you better have something solid to back it up."

"I know." I sighed, swirling the ice in my nearly empty Diet Coke. "But if someone is targeting people in our community, I need to find out who and why. And I can't ignore any leads."

The two men exchanged glances, understanding the depth of my resolve.

"I'll back you up," Owen said quietly. "As long as you promise to be careful. This town... It's full of secrets."

"Every town is," Shawn added with a knowing look.

I nodded, grateful for their support and information.

"Thanks, both of you. Just... keep this between us for now. I need to dig deeper. But why would they target Albert? And why would their house and his delivery truck have been ransacked?" I asked.

"Albert?" Owen mused, squinting slightly as if trying to remember something important. "Didn't he used to work on a project connected to the land next to the Leisure Center, before he started deliveries?"

Shawn nodded.

"Yeah, back when they were still doing some preliminary surveys and all. Supposedly found something of historical value, which added more complications to Louise's development plans." He threw out a hand. "That was years ago, though."

I tapped my fingers on the bar, thinking.

"Years ago, maybe the property wasn't worth as much? So maybe he had something they wanted? Documents or proofs that could either aid their projects or be detrimental to them?" I asked.

Owen leaned in and lowered his voice. "Rumor has it that when Albert was surveying the land, he stumbled across old town records that indicated some part of the Leisure Center land was preserved for public use—a green space of sorts. That would make it impossible to ever develop it, even if zoning laws changed."

"So that's why there's the extra lot next to the Leisure Center," I said. "I know Mama wanted to see if she could have the village turn it into some sort of walking trail so the seniors could use it for outdoor exercise. But after all these years?" I shook my head.

None of what they were saying was adding up. I continued to listen, though. That was how journalism worked for me. I would gather all the information and weed through the details to see which ones would stick, and that would lead me to the rabbit hole I'd descend.

"As for Marianne, there might've been correspondence or some sort of proof that Tara had in her house that could implicate her in something shady. Or perhaps evidence that Marianne had attempted to bribe or pressure officials to get her ball moved to the art district," Shawn added.

"If Albert had copies of those old records or any other evidence, they'd want it, right?" I said, connecting the dots. "Maybe they thought he was going to use it against them."

"Exactly," Shawn whispered. "Daphne would want it to either forge or destroy, ensuring her development moved forward. And Marianne would just want anything that painted her in a bad light out of the picture."

Owen sighed deeply. "This town might be festive on the surface, but beneath all the tinsel and lights, there are always shadows."

"I just hope I can bring some of those shadows to light," I murmured.. The puzzle pieces were slowly falling into place, and I was intent on seeing the full picture.

Owen and Shawn exchanged a glance, as though a silent understanding was passing between them.

"Ah, Cassidy," Owen began, drumming his fingers on the bar. "She's quite the go-getter, isn't she? Always looking for a good deal, that one."

"She's tried to get her hands on more than a few prime properties in town. A bit too eager, if you ask me." Shawn smirked.

I raised an eyebrow, intrigued.

"Is there something specific about her dealings with the Hardens?" I asked.

Owen leaned closer. In a lowered voice, he said, "Well, rumor has it she made an offer to buy a piece of land Albert owned. Not the one connected to the Leisure Center but another spot. Prime real estate. But Albert never wanted to sell it. Said it had sentimental value."

"And Tara," Shawn chimed in. "She reportedly had some heated discussions with Cassidy at a few town meetings. Cassidy wanted to transform a piece of public land into a new luxury housing development, and Tara was vehemently against it."

"Where is the piece of property?" I asked.

"Up in the art district." Shawn shrugged.

"But it's just talk, Violet," Owen added with caution. "Cassidy's aggressive in business, sure, but murder? It's a leap."

Not when it comes to money and lifestyle, I thought.

"Another round on me," I said to the bartender, circling my finger in the air as I walked out the door.

CHAPTER EIGHT

A s I began my walk down the sidewalk, I tried to figure out what my next move would be.

I really needed to know if there was foul play involving the Hardens, but my curiosity about Tara's luncheon was still piqued. Even if Tara wasn't murdered, there was still the sinister little land development issue that might be a huge news story or an exposé.

The salty air carried the crisp scent of fall with it, and the rustling of the dry leaves under my feet played a rhythm against the sounds of the waves crashing onto the shore.

The Thanksgiving decorations by the seaside were different than the ones downtown. The shops along the ocean leaned toward the more rustic and homey side—pumpkins, hay bales, and autumnal wreaths adorned every storefront, preparing to make way for the more vibrant and glittery adornments of Christmas. Yet, amidst this peaceful setting, the thought of the mystery I was delving into brought a chill that wasn't just from the cool sea breeze.

My phone rang, and I stopped in front of Freedom Diner to get it out of my bag.

Pulling my phone out, I saw Darren's name light up the screen.

"Hey, Darren," I said and smiled. It was early for me to hear from him, but I liked it.

"Violet"—his voice was hushed—"can you meet me at the lighthouse? I've got some information on the Hardens."

I glanced toward the sea. The lighthouse stood tall and imposing in the distance, its white and red stripes contrasting starkly against the grayish blue of the approaching winter sky.

"I'm just leaving your jiggle joint. I've got some information too." The smell coming from Freedom Diner made my stomach rumble. "I'm walking up to Freedom Diner. I'll grab some burger baskets and be right down."

As I began my walk, I smelled that crisp scent of fall on the salty air, and the rustling of the dry leaves under my feet played a rhythm that echoed in the quiet town. The waves, a bit more aggressive due to the changing season, crashed against the shoreline, adding to the backdrop of soothing sounds.

When I pushed open the door to Freedom Diner, the welcoming aroma of grilled patties and freshly baked buns washed over me. The smell was even more enticing when juxtaposed against the salty air outside.

Nate Lustig, the diner owner, who had a friendly face and a perpetually cheerful disposition, greeted me from behind the counter.

"Hey there, Violet! What can I get for you today?" he asked.

I glanced at the menu overhead, although I already knew what I wanted.

"Two of your classic burger baskets, please, Nate. With extra fries and burger sauce." I smiled because he knew how much I loved dipping my fries in his special homemade sauce.

Nate began to punch in my order but hesitated a moment.

"Might be a bit of a wait today. Chief Strickland just put in a big order. Seems the station's a hive of activity with the double homicide and all," he said.

I blinked, trying to mask my surprise at his mention of homicide.

"Double homicide?" I echoed, careful to keep my voice casual.

Nate leaned in slightly and lowered his voice. "Word's just come out. Albert and Tara Harden were murdered." He shook his head, his brow furrowed with genuine concern. "Terrible thing. This town... We're not used to such tragedy. And she was such a good cook."

Feeling a sudden coldness despite the diner's warm ambiance, I nodded.

"It's shocking. I can't believe it." I purposely left out my presence at both crime scenes.

"They were good folks," Nate continued. "Always stopped by here for their morning coffee. Can't imagine who would want to do this to them."

Trying to shift the focus, I asked, "Any idea why Chief Strickland ordered so much food?"

"You know the force. Any time there's a big case, they're working round the clock. Guess they need fuel to keep going. Good for business." Nate shrugged, his jovial demeanor returning.

"Well, when you can, get those burgers ready." I smiled weakly.

"You got it, Violet," Nate added as I turned to find a seat to wait.

I sat down on one of the barstools that was butted up to the old diner's counter and got my notebook out. In it, I wrote down everything I knew about Marianne, Louise, and Cassidy, though Betsy was in the back of my mind.

Gazing at the scribbled motives in my notebook, I felt the significance of the task ahead. There was a tangled web to unravel, and it seemed to point back at these three women. Each motive provided a lead, a starting point to begin my deeper investigation.

First, Marianne.

The art district was now on my radar. If Marianne had been pushing for her annual ball to be relocated there, that area might have evidence or individuals who knew more. I could visit the art district, mingle with the locals and artists, and gather any whispers about Marianne's ambitions and her disagreements with Tara.

The idea of a significant revenue stream from her ball had potential. I had to find out if she had any financial troubles that could've made that shift more of a desperate move than a simple preference. And then there were the rumors, the softer side of the story. Was there an incident between her and Tara that wasn't public knowledge? A personal vendetta could often drive people further than financial motives could.

What about Louise?

I circled her name a few times and then started to scribble down her possible motives.

The land next to the Leisure Center was a glaring beacon. Perhaps visiting the town's planning office could provide some insight into Louise's failed proposals and the exact nature of Tara's objections.

Maybe there were other investors involved, ones who weren't as patient as Louise.

If anyone had a lot of financial gain in the village, it would be Cassidy.

I needed to learn more about her recent real estate transactions and if any of them had clashed with the Hardens' interests.

A visit to the local real estate office, or better yet, a tour of one of her properties as if I were a potential buyer, might offer an avenue to gather more information.

And in all of this, Betsy's name still echoed in the back of my mind— her odd behavior and her presence on the invite list.

I'd need to approach her again, so stopping by the florist to get Mama a new fall arrangement for the Leisure Center's entrance just might be the thing.

Each name on my list seemed to open doors to different avenues of the investigation. I knew this was just the beginning, but I was determined to get to the bottom of the case. With the leads laid out before me, it was time to pound the pavement and chase the truth.

"Here you go," Nate said, stacking one to-go box on top of another. "Tell Darren I added a few extra pickles on his."

"How did you know it was for Darren?" I wondered and smiled, knowing our little secret romance was no longer a secret.

But I hoped our Merry Maker secret was still under wraps.

Speaking of the Merry Maker, I still hadn't found a good place to end the Thanksgiving Festival. Darren hadn't been able to help, and now with these two homicides, my time was limited because I had to do the investigative reporting.

Had to!

Reaching the lighthouse, I found the door slightly ajar. Using the toe of my shoe, I pushed it open.

"Darren?" I called out.

"Up here," his voice echoed from the top.

I walked through the house portion and soon found myself climbing the winding staircase. The faint smells of old wood, salt, and fried burgers met my nose.

The lighthouse's circular windows gave fleeting glimpses of the town and the sea as I made my way up. By the time I reached the top, my heart was racing from more than just the climb.

The panoramic view of Holiday Junction was breathtaking, even if I had seen it a dozen times before, and Darren didn't look so bad either.

He stood near the railing, a folder in his hands and a serious expression on his face.

"Tara and Albert were—" he started to say in his somber voice.

"Murdered," I interrupted and put the boxes of food on the table he had up here. "And I have a few suspects already."

I wasn't yet able to tell him all about Tara, so I gave him a quick rundown on how I'd gone over to Tara's and found the body.

"Also, your dad had all his resources at the Leisure Center, so he had me take photos of the scene," I said, noticing his shock that his dad had done something totally unlike him.

I tapped on my phone screen a few times, getting the photos to come up, and handed him the phone.

"Swipe left," I told him before I opened the boxes of food and found which one was mine. I set his box in front of him. "Here." I reached into my bag and handed him the notebook that I used for stories. Today, I was going to use it for the festival activities.

I chowed down on the contents of my burger basket. I practically finished all my food before he even got the condiments and extra pickles on his burger, since he took so long going over everything I'd showed him.

"I wish you hadn't shown me all this." He looked up, appearing less excited than I thought he would be.

"Marianne Drew came to see Diffy today, and she's afraid she's going to be named a suspect. Now that you've given me the information we've requested from Dad before he's shared it with us, I can't use it." Darren pushed back his to-go box. "I can't eat."

"Darren, I'm sorry, it's just that I had no—" I was going to really apologize, but I stopped myself. "Wait. You could've said all of this and shoved away the information instead of looking at all of it."

"I didn't know you had found Tara. I didn't know Marianne was going there for a luncheon, and by the looks of the photo of Tara's calendar and the information about needing to change the ball, I'm leery of what Marianne's said." He tugged his lips together.

"What did she say?" I asked.

"I can't tell you." He got up and walked back and forth, stopping briefly and looking out across the sea as if it would give him clarity. "I can't discuss this with you. If I still have any client–attorney privilege, I need to invoke that now."

"Fine." I grabbed the notebook, shut it, and placed it and my phone in my bag. "If you don't want help, that's fine."

This was a line Darren and I'd never crossed. Since the day I'd met him, he was always so forthcoming and straightforward and never tight-lipped.

"Regardless of whatever we have going on here..." I wagged a finger between us. As they said where I came from, the tension was thicker than molasses in January. "We still have to figure out the Merry Maker."

"Yeah. Yeah. What if we meet up again tonight during the bonfire?" he suggested in a clearly insincere way.

Never in my life was I so happy to hear my phone ring.

It was Fern Banks. Strange.

"Hey, I've got to go. I need to take this." I really didn't need to take the call, but it was a great time to get out of here. The atmosphere held a tension I'd not felt since Darren and I had started dating in public, and I was really good at fleeing.

I gave him a quick peck on the cheek and headed down the steps as quickly as I could without getting vertigo from going around and around.

I hit the green answer button before I got to the bottom of the stairs so I didn't lose the call.

"Hello?" I heard Fern's voice coming through the phone. "Violet? You there? Hello?"

"Hey," I said, pushing through the door of the lighthouse and letting the late-afternoon sun hit my eyes.

"Oh, you sound off," she said.

"Do you want to meet at Cup of Cheer?" I asked as I walked down the sidewalk back along the seaside toward Cup of Cheer.

"You must be desperate to talk to someone." She laughed, joking about how we were neither exactly friends nor enemies. "See you soon."

CHAPTER NINE

Cup of Cheer was an inviting shop, and the moment I stepped in, I felt enveloped in the warm embrace of fall. The aroma of spiced cider and roasted tea leaves filled the air, creating an intoxicating blend that immediately made me feel all cozy.

The gentle hum of conversations, the clinking of mugs and teacups, and the occasional delighted laugh from a corner told me that this was the place to be in Holiday Junction today, especially with the Cider Tasting underway.

I had hoped to find a quiet spot to chat with Fern, but with the Cider Tasting event in full swing, every table was occupied. Regulars and newcomers alike had turned up, wanting to sample and savor the different cider flavors the Cup of Cheer had on offer.

As I maneuvered my way through the cozy space, I noticed several stations set up for the cider tasting. There were large glass dispensers, each filled with a different shade of amber liquid, signifying the variety of ciders. A small placard in front of each dispenser detailed the type of apple used, the spices incorporated, and even the recommended tea pairings.

Residents of Holiday Junction eagerly filled their mugs, swirled the cider, and breathed in its aroma and then took a careful sip, often followed by an appreciative nod or a thoughtful frown.

The wall with the hooks, from which teacups hung for customers to take and fill up, was a spectacle in itself. Today, many people had chosen mugs that seemed to resonate with the autumnal spirit. Some had hues of burnt orange, deep maroon, and soft gold. Certain mugs even had festive designs: dancing leaves, pumpkins, or sayings like "Fall in love with Autumn" painted on them.

Tables were adorned with small vases holding twigs that bore crimson and gold leaves, while miniature pumpkins were artistically placed amidst the trays, adding to the autumn vibe.

The fireplace, positioned at the center of the room, crackled and popped, casting a warm, flickering glow across the patrons, its smoky scent mingling with the spicy notes of the cider.

I scanned the sea of faces, looking for a familiar mane of perfectly styled hair or the glint of a beauty queen's tiara, but Fern hadn't arrived yet. Realizing that finding a seat might prove to be a Herculean task, I approached the tea bar, thinking that perhaps I could snag a couple of stools there until a table became free. The idea of sipping warm cider and discussing the latest town events with Fern by the bar didn't sound too bad.

I didn't see Fern here yet, so I decided it was time to put aside the murder investigation and focus on the *Junction Journal*.

The cider event was on my agenda for the day.

Camera in hand, I made my way to a particularly lively group of people who were enthusiastically discussing the various ciders. I approached a tall, broad-shouldered man with salt-and-pepper hair, noticing the way his eyes sparkled as he spoke about the cider he was sampling.

"Excuse me, sir," I began, flashing my friendliest reporter smile. "I'm Violet from the *Junction Journal*. Would you mind if I took a photo of you enjoying the cider tasting? We're doing a feature, and I'd love to get your thoughts."

He looked surprised then beamed. "Well, I'd be delighted! Name's

Benjamin Hartley." With that, he lifted his mug, took a deep sip, and let out an exaggerated sigh of satisfaction. I clicked the camera just in time to capture his wide smile and slightly raised eyebrows, which expressed his delight.

"And how are you finding the tasting?" I prompted, pen poised over my notebook.

"Divine!" he exclaimed, gesturing with his mug toward the different cider dispensers. "Never thought I'd be a cider man, but these flavors! The apple cinnamon one? A true game-changer."

Nearby, a young woman with a pixie haircut and freckle-dotted cheeks overheard our conversation and chimed in, "I second that! The blend of spices they've used this year is just spot-on." She extended a hand. "Daisy Miller."

I jotted down their names and their comments and then asked, "Do you have a favorite?"

Daisy cradled her mug close and took a deep whiff. "Mmm, the spiced cranberry apple cider is my top pick. It's like the whole fall season in a mug!"

Benjamin nodded. "Can't argue with that, although I have a soft spot for the classic pumpkin spiced blend."

As I wrote down their insights, an elderly lady with striking silver hair pulled back in a tight bun gestured for me to come over. "Young lady, you mustn't forget the maple pecan cider," she said in a tone that suggested both authority and warmth.

"Of course!" I replied. "And may I have your name, ma'am?"

"Jean Whitmore. And let me tell you, dear, this maple pecan is like a cozy blanket on a chilly day." She tapped her fingernail against the ceramic mug.

I laughed, scribbling her comment down. "Thank you, Mrs. Whitmore."

The door chimed softly behind me as I settled into one of the leather conversation chairs, but a quick glance showed it wasn't Fern who entered. I refocused on pulling out my notepad and pencil.

Moments later, the scent of a floral perfume announced Fern's arrival, and she emerged from behind a display of specialty teas.

"Violet!" she exclaimed, her voice as crisp and refined as her appearance. "I'm so glad you could make it."

When I looked up, I couldn't help but be taken aback for a moment by how put together Fern appeared, even inside a bustling shop.

"Fern, you look lovely. What's the occasion?" I asked, looking at her dress.

She gracefully settled into the chair across from me, her lace dress rustling softly.

"Oh, I just wanted to look my best," she replied with a playful wink, removing her sunglasses and revealing bright, expectant eyes. "Now, I have a favor to ask."

Before I could reply, the sound of a clinking tray caught my attention.

Mrs. Stevens, the owner of Cup of Cheer, approached with a knowing smile.

"Violet, dear, I thought you might like to try our signature autumn spice cider. I'm so glad you're covering the tasting for the *Junction Journal*," she said.

"That's right," I replied, my senses immediately captivated by the aromatic steam wafting from the cups, one of which I took. "Thank you, Mrs. Stevens."

"My pleasure, dear. Just make sure you capture the essence of our little shop," she said with a wink of her own. Then she moved on to tend to another group of patrons.

"It seems like you have quite the influence around here," Fern said, her eyes twinkling with amusement.

I chuckled, taking a sip of the cider. The warmth of cinnamon and a hint of nutmeg danced on my tongue.

"It's just part of the job," I replied modestly. "Now, what did you want to talk about?"

"Well," she began, nervously twirling a strand of her black hair with her fingers, "I want to ask your mama about pageant classes."

I raised an eyebrow in surprise.

Fern sighed, her gaze momentarily lost in the swirls of her own cider.

"I respect her. She has this elegance and poise that I want to emulate. And I've heard from many that she used to give pageant coaching back in the day." Fern had done her research.

"That's true," I replied, recalling the many trophies and sashes Mama proudly displayed at home from pageants she'd made me enter when I was a kid, though she'd never pushed me to compete to the extent that Fern had. She still held a few pageant titles, and when I moved here, she was Miss Holiday Junction. "But why come to me?"

"Because, Violet," Fern replied, leaning in with earnestness evident in her eyes, "your mama respects you. And I think if you talk to her, she might consider it."

I took another sip of my cider, mulling over Fern's words.

"I can't promise anything, Fern, but I'll certainly mention it to her," I told her, even though I knew Mama would jump at the chance to have Fern come in there and teach classes.

"Thank you, Violet. That means the world to me." She clasped her hands, her face brightening with gratitude.

Fern took a dainty sip of her cider before lowering the cup and giving me a sly smile. "Speaking of relationships, I've heard a little rumor about you and Darren making it official."

I felt my cheeks warm up, and the steam from the cup no longer seemed to be the sole culprit.

"Where'd you hear that?" I tried to sound nonchalant, but the hints of a smile at the corners of my mouth probably betrayed me.

"It's a small town. Besides"—she tilted her head playfully—"you two have been seen together quite a lot lately. What's going on?"

I searched for a response that wasn't too revealing because no matter what I said, Fern would hear what she wanted to tell people, and Darren and I had been really on the down-low about it.

Just then, my phone rang, saving me from further probing. I glanced at the screen, and the name Mama flashed across it.

"Excuse me, Fern, I have to take this. It's Mama." I offered her an apologetic smile.

"Of course," Fern replied. "Mention me." She pointed at herself.

"Hello, Mama?" I answered the call, grateful for the timely interruption.

Millie Kay's voice was a mixture of distress and agitation.

"Violet, honey, Diffy Delk just called me. They're saying it's murder now. Can you believe it? The whole thing with the Hardens!" Mama cried out.

"Mama, are you okay?" I asked, not letting her know that Darren had already been told me the Hardens were murdered.

She took a deep breath, trying to calm herself.

"Well, as okay as I can be. But Diffy wants me to come down to his office to give a statement. Says it's better to have everything documented early on. I'm not sure what he thinks I can tell him." Mama's voice cracked. "Do you think they suspect me, since Albert was found in my Leisure Center?"

"I don't think so. I mean, Darren and I were with you most of the time. But don't worry, Mama. Just tell him what you know, or in this case, what you don't know. And I'll come meet you there," I said, gathering my things in my bag.

I was satisfied that the photos and the customers I'd talked to had given me enough to create the feature.

"I'm at home, so I can jump in my golf cart and meet you there," she replied, though I could hear the uncertainty in her voice.

"I'll meet you at Diffy's office. I'm coming from Cup of Cheer, so it'll be a minute," I said.

I could almost hear her nodding through the phone.

"Thank you, honey. I'll see you there," Mama said.

After I hung up, I turned to Fern, who was watching me with a mix of concern and curiosity. "Sorry, Fern, something's come up. I need to go."

Fern's playful demeanor had shifted. "Everything okay?"

I hesitated. "Just some family stuff to sort out. I'll call you later?"

She nodded. "Of course. Take care, and if you need anything, just let me know."

I smiled, appreciating her concern. "Thanks, Fern. I'll keep that in mind." With a quick wave, I prepared to leave Cup of Cheer, my mind racing with the implications of the new turn in the investigation.

As I was about to head toward the door, Fern leaned in closer, her voice dropping to a conspiratorial whisper. "Did I hear your mama say 'Hardens'?"

"Yeah." I sighed, picking up my bag and tossing it over my shoulder.

"Shame." She shook her head. "I loved watching Tara Harden's YouTube cooking show. I was hoping to get her to the pageant school for a lesson."

I paused and turned back to face her, my curiosity piqued. "YouTube?"

She leaned back with a smirk, clearly enjoying being the bearer of juicy news. "Oh, honey, it's taken off like a wildfire. Apparently, some celebrity shared one of her videos, and now she's got thousands and thousands of subscribers. There's even talk of her getting her own show on a big network. There *was*."

My eyebrows rose in surprise. Tara's YouTube channel was news to me.

"Really? That's impressive," I said as my mind whirled with possible new motives for her murder.

Fern nodded, her eyes gleaming with mischief. "Yes, but with newfound fame come newfound enemies. Lots of them. Jealousy's a powerful motivator, Violet. Just something to chew on with everything going on."

I considered the implications of Fern's words. "Thanks for the tip, Fern. I'll keep it in mind."

She winked.

"Always here to help, especially since I know a lot of people here and it helps me get in the door at the Leisure Center," she said, giving me her reason for the gossip. "I've got more where that came from too." She was talking about gossip and the Hardens.

"Do you want to come with me? Afterward, I have to go to the Hippity Hoppity for the pumpkin patch." I wanted to hear everything Fern had to say.

"Sure." She jumped up, her dress shifting as she maneuvered her sweater on. "I'm all dolled up, so I might'swell be seen."

CHAPTER TEN

The vibrant autumn sun cast a golden hue over Holiday Park, turning the seaside town of Holiday Junction into a picturesque scene straight out of a postcard. Fern and I hurried along the sidewalk, our heels clicking rhythmically against the stone, underscoring the town's anticipation for the upcoming Thanksgiving festivities.

As we approached the park, our senses were immediately engulfed by the myriad of colors and scents that only fall could offer. Every tree seemed to compete in a dazzling display of reds, oranges, and yellows. The ground was a carpet of fallen leaves, rustling with every gust of wind, and each step we took felt like we were walking on a path made of gold.

Vendors had set up stalls throughout the park, their wares displayed on rustic wooden tables draped in deep maroon and burnt-orange cloths. The sellers were peddling everything from hand-knit scarves to freshly baked pies. Warm scents of cinnamon, nutmeg, and pumpkin wafted through the air, inviting visitors to sample the culinary delights.

In the center of the park, the massive fountain bubbled over, its water shimmering under the sun, bordered by huge pots overflowing with chrysanthemums in shades of white, yellow, and rust. The amphitheater was wrapped in garlands of dried corn and marigolds, ready to host the various performances scheduled for the season. A large, beautifully designed poster announced the Leaf Dance, the image's deep-green and gold lettering standing out against a backdrop of cascading autumn leaves. In my head, I made a mental note: *I need to speak with Vern about creating that sign for the Merry Maker.*

We slowed our pace, momentarily getting distracted by the allure of the vendors and their offerings. Fern's eyes sparkled as she gestured toward a stall selling intricately designed jewelry. "We should come back here later," she whispered, already planning our post-meeting spree.

"I agree." I smiled, admiring a gorgeous pair of handmade earrings. "But let's hurry now. We have more pressing matters."

As we continued through the park, our budding camaraderie became evident to me. It felt like Fern and I were two friends catching up rather than just acquaintances.

I cleared my throat, thinking now might be a good time to gather more information. "Speaking of the Hardens, do you know Daphne Marsh? Or have any idea if she had any involvement with Tara's YouTube show?"

Fern thought for a moment, her forehead creasing slightly.

"Daphne? I've met her a few times at social gatherings. As for any dealings with Tara, I'm not certain, but in this town, it's hard to believe that they haven't crossed paths at some point." She made a great point.

Her words left me pondering as we approached Central Square. The gravity of the investigation still on my mind and, I imagined, hers as well.

"You know, now that you mention it, I'd love to get in front of Daphne myself. Not for anything related to the investigation"—she chuckled lightly, adjusting the strap of her purse on her shoulder—"but I've been thinking of approaching her about donating some items from the thrift shop for our pageant classes."

"Oh?" I raised an eyebrow, intrigued. "Were you thinking about seeing her soon?"

"Is tomorrow too soon?" Fern grinned, and so did I. "I'll pick you up in the morning, and we will go the thrift store—that is, if Millie Kay agrees that I can have pageant classes there."

"If you give her ten percent of the class fee, I think you'll have a deal," I said and held my hand out while we were walking.

Fern pondered the idea for about a split second.

"Deal." She took my hand and gave it a real hard shake as we entered the building where Diffy's office was located.

The bell over the door to Diffy's office chimed gently as Fern and I walked in, immediately announcing our presence. The office was a strange amalgamation of stuffiness and quirkiness, an accurate reflection of the man himself.

The first thing that caught my eye, before even Diffy or Mama, was Dave the Rooster. There he was, perched proudly on a platform in the corner, his crimson comb and wattles contrasting sharply with his golden feathers.

He watched us with an uncanny intelligence in his eyes, as if daring us to question his presence in a lawyer's office. The bird looked well cared for, with his shiny feathers and an aura of confidence that seemed to say, *"I know I'm out of place, and I don't care."*

Dave wasn't just a rooster. Like Mayor Paisley, he had a real job. Dave was actually a security rooster at the Holiday Junction Airport. But he didn't have to work every day—the airport was so small that it was open on only certain days during the week.

"Ah, Violet! Fern! Good to see you both. You've already met Dave," Diffy said with a grin, gesturing toward the rooster while getting up from his grand oak desk.

The desk, in stark contrast to the rest of the modest room, seemed more suited to a grand boardroom than this cramped office space. It was almost comical to see Diffy, in his unmistakably polyester suit, sitting behind that desk.

Pictures of Dave in various stances decorated the walls—this rooster was clearly a cherished pet, not just a random office fixture.

I stifled a giggle, remembering the photo of Diffy I'd seen online. He certainly had used some kind of photo magic; his actual hairline seemed to have retreated farther than the beaches at low tide.

Beside the desk, in a far less ostentatious chair, sat Mama, Millie Kay. She seemed a little anxious, her eyes darting between Diffy and us.

"Violet," she said, her voice carrying a hint of relief.

"Hey, Mama," I replied, giving her a reassuring nod.

Diffy cleared his throat, which drew the attention back to him. "Shall we get started?"

Before I could respond, Fern, ever the opportunist, pointed at Dave and said, "Now there's a creature who knows how to command a room. I could use someone like him at the pageant school."

"Well, Dave certainly has a unique presence. But for now, he's committed to his duties at the airport and as my esteemed office companion," Diffy chuckled.

"Pageant school?" Mama's eyebrows rose in surprise, her interest clearly piqued.

Fern, pouncing on her chance as usual, clasped her hands together and leaned forward in her chair.

"Yes, Ms. Millie Kay. I've been wanting to start a pageant school for the young ladies of our town. I believe there's so much untapped potential, and I want to provide them with the skills and confidence they need to shine." She beamed.

Mama tilted her head thoughtfully.

"And you're thinking of the Leisure Center as a venue?" Mama asked.

"Exactly!" Fern beamed again, clearly excited. "It has the perfect space for rehearsals and classes. Plus, with its location and reputation, I believe it will attract many interested participants."

I watched the exchange, impressed by Fern's drive and passion. For all her quirks and ambitions, she had a genuine desire to uplift others, which I found admirable.

Diffy, clearly amused by the sudden turn of conversation in his office, rubbed his chin thoughtfully.

"Well, if you ladies decide to go ahead with this venture, I'd be more than happy to draft a contract for you. Or better yet, have Darren Strickland do it. He's been doing a stellar job clerking here while attending law school." Diffy wouldn't miss out on an opportunity when he saw one either.

My heart skipped a beat at the mention of Darren's name. Before I could react, Mama shot me a quick, knowing look and wiggled her eyebrows suggestively. It was a look that said, "I know what's going on between you two." I felt my cheeks flush and gazed at the floor, attempting to hide my embarrassment.

Diffy, oblivious to the silent exchange between Mama and me, continued, "Darren's got a keen eye for detail. He'd make sure everything's in order."

"So, what do you say, Ms. Millie Kay? Are you open to discussing this possibility?" Fern, seizing the moment, extended her hand to Mama.

Mama regarded her for a moment, looking thoughtful. After what felt like an eternity, she nodded. "I'm willing to listen."

Fern grinned, her excitement palpable. "Wonderful!"

"Okay, okay," I interjected, feeling the day's commitments pressing on me. "Diffy, we really need to discuss the reason we're here. I've got a tight schedule with the pumpkin patch event at the Hippity Hoppity, and there's still the matter of the Hardens' murder investigation to get to."

Diffy leaned back in his swivel chair, the slight creaking sound making a sharp contrast to the earlier lighthearted discussion.

"Ah, right," he sighed, removing his glasses and rubbing the bridge of his nose. "The unfortunate matter at hand. Millie Kay, I understand that Albert Harden was found at your Leisure Center?"

Mama shifted uncomfortably.

"Yes, that's right. It was such a shock," she said with a frown.

Diffy nodded sympathetically.

"I can only imagine. Now, I'm representing Marianne Drew in this matter. Chief Strickland informed me that she was supposed to attend a luncheon at Tara's today. Do you know anything about that?" he asked.

Mama pondered for a moment, her fingers tracing the edge of the armrest.

"Marianne did mention a luncheon to me a few days ago when she came into the Leisure Center. She was excited about some potential business opportunities with Tara. But as for the specifics, I wasn't privy to them," she noted.

Fern shifted in her seat, too, clearly feeling out of place in the more serious discussion, but she remained silent, her gaze bouncing from Mama to Diffy to me.

"And you didn't see or hear anything unusual at the Leisure Center before the discovery?" Diffy inquired, his voice soft but probing.

Mama shook her head, her face etched with concern. "Nothing at all. I wish I had. It might've changed things."

Diffy sighed, scribbling something down on his notepad. "All right, I'll relay this information to the chief. We need to ensure Marianne's side of the story is clear and that she's not unjustly implicated in any of this."

Before I left, a nagging thought crossed my mind. Turning to Diffy, I asked, "Did Marianne mention anything about moving the Mistletoe Masquerade Ball? I've heard some chatter around town."

Diffy adjusted his tie, looking thoughtful for a moment.

"She did mention it in passing. Something about finding a new venue that would accommodate more people and bring in additional revenue for the town," he said.

"That's why she stopped by the Leisure Center," Mama added.

"And did Tara Harden have anything to do with that?" I pressed, curious about any possible connections between the two women.

Diffy hesitated for a moment, clearly trying to figure out how much he could share.

"It's complicated. From what Marianne shared with me, Tara did express interest in collaborating for the ball." His lips were tight.

I nodded, filing that piece of information away. Every bit of knowledge could prove crucial in piecing together the puzzle of what had transpired.

"Thank you, Diffy," I said, glancing once more at the proud rooster perched on its platform, "for everything."

Diffy smiled, a hint of weariness in his eyes. "Just doing my job, Violet. Stay safe out there, and keep me updated if you learn anything new."

"Will do." I gathered my things, as did Fern and Mama.

When we all got outside and away from Diffy, I stopped them.

"Mama, did Marianne mention anything about Tara and her cooking show on YouTube?" I asked to jar Mama's memory.

"She mentioned something about cameras coming in, but then she waved it off, telling me that if she decided to rent the Leisure Center, she'd fill me in on the details."

Mama had made enough of a connection between Marianne Drew and Tara Harden that I knew Marianne had to stay on my list of people to see.

CHAPTER ELEVEN

The ranch was on the beach and had what looked to be about five acres with a barn built in the back. I had no clue the ranch's owners had all the things they did on the adjoining property when I came here a year ago during another investigation.

"I can't believe you didn't know about the market Millard has back here," Fern said, stopping briefly to put her shoes back on once we reached the sidewalk that led us past the horse barn that I'd been to.

Walking along the beach before we got here was a nice way to clear my mind and consider what to ask Millard Ramsey about Albert Harden working for her. Mama never told me how she'd gotten the information for the ranch to deliver the milk she needed for the Friendsgiving dishes.

The path leading up to the pumpkin patch was lined with vibrant orange and golden marigolds, their petals rustling softly in the sea breeze. The salty air mixed with the earthy scent of pumpkins and hay, creating an ambience that felt both fresh and rustic. The sound of children's laughter filled the air, their excitement contagious.

The pumpkin patch unfolded before us like an autumnal wonderland. Rows upon rows of pumpkins lay spread out, ranging from the tiniest little gourds perfect for a child's hand to enormous ones that would require a wheelbarrow to transport.

Scarecrows, decked out in flannel shirts and denim overalls, stood guard amidst the sea of orange, their straw hats casting playful shadows on the ground.

Without hesitation, I reached inside my bag and took out my camera to get some good snapshots for the event's feature in the *Junction Journal*.

"I thought we were here to get answers," Fern said in a snotty voice.

"We are, but I have to report on it as well," I told her and then turned to the left, where a

cluster of children surrounded an artist at the face-painting booth.

Bright colors flashed as brushes danced over eager faces, transforming the children into tigers, fairies, and even a few miniature pumpkins. Nearby, parents and kids worked together at carving stations, scooping out pumpkin guts with gusto and carefully etching out intricate designs. I took a moment to snap a few photos of a particularly diligent father-son duo whose brows were furrowed in concentration.

The scents of cinnamon and apple wafted over from a nearby stall where a woman was handing out samples of warm cider. As I approached, she offered me a cup with a welcoming smile. The first sip was heavenly—the perfect balance of sweet and tart with that unmistakable kick of spices.

Fern nudged me and pointed toward another booth where kids were meticulously painting their pumpkins. Bright blues, purples, and greens contrasted beautifully against the natural orange hue. Every child seemed to have their own vision, whether it was a multicolored abstract masterpiece or a detailed portrait of a beloved pet.

Farther off, hayrides were in full swing. Families clambered onto wagons filled with stacks upon stacks of hay, and the passengers' faces lit up with anticipation as they were taken on a leisurely tour around the ranch's expansive property. The rhythmic sound of hooves against the earth and the occasional whinny of a horse added to the place's pastoral feel.

As I snapped away with my camera, capturing candid moments of joy, Fern chatted with some of the parents, taking notes for potential leads into the world of pageantry. Despite the underlying tension of my investigation, it was hard not to get swept up in the infectious merriment of the pumpkin patch festival. Fern would use the opportunity to find any potential customers.

"Hey, Violet! Everything good? Need anything?" A friendly voice interrupted my focus as I was framing my next shot.

I looked up and saw Tito Ramsey, Millard's tall and broad-shouldered son, smiling down at me. His dark hair, a shade or two lighter than his mother's, fluttered in the autumn breeze. The last time I'd seen him, he was playing the Headless Horseman at the annual Halloweenie festival.

"Hi, Tito," I told him warmly. "Actually, I was hoping to have a word with your mom. Is she around?"

My phone chirped a message. I ignored it.

Tito pointed toward a large, festively decorated tent where a woman with shoulder-length brown hair was overseeing a couple of workers arranging pumpkins on a display.

"There she is. Head of the operation, as always," he said.

"Thanks," I said, nodding at him and proceeded toward the tent.

Walking over, I took my phone out to see who'd texted me. It was Mama.

Mama: *I remember what Marianne said about that camera thing. Really, it was Tara who mentioned something about the lighting in the Leisure Center.*

Me: *What?*

Mama: *Tara had a show, and she wanted to go live on it during the Mistletoe Masquerade Ball and make cornbread dressing.*

My mouth watered.

Me: *What happened?*

Mama: *Marianne said the light wasn't good for that, but the natural light at that hour on top of the mountain in the art district would look amazing on the show. But Tara told her Albert wouldn't go for it, so Marianne had to get it out of her head.*

Me: *Did Marianne show up at the Leisure Center for her appointment?*

Mama: *No, ain't talked to her since.*

Me: *I'll call you soon.*

I tried to gulp back the theory that a little television show run by Tara had hurt Marianne's ego and status in the community, but Marianne had a big ego. The incident Mama described would have been enough for Marianne to try to talk Albert out of letting Tara host the show. When he didn't agree, a little pushy-push did the trick.

As I approached Millard, I took in her appearance. The sun highlighted the streaks of silver in her brown hair, and her face was lined with the wisdom of someone who had seen many pumpkin seasons come and go.

"Millard," I began, extending a hand, "it's lovely to see you again."

She turned, her face lighting up with recognition.

"Violet! It's been too long. What brings you to the Hippity Hoppity today?" she asked.

I hesitated for a moment to frame my question carefully.

"Actually, I'm here not just for the article I'm writing about the pumpkin patch but also because I wanted to ask you something. Do you know who recently inquired about getting milk deliveries up at the art district?" I asked.

"Hmm, there've been a few inquiries. The art district folks love fresh produce, and our milk is popular. But if you're referring to someone specific, I'm drawing a blank. Why?" Millard's expression turned thoughtful. "Or is this about Albert?" She frowned.

"Well, I'm trying to piece together information that might give Matthew Strickland some insight. I understand from the chamber records we keep at the office that someone had asked Albert if they'd deliver up there, and they got into a little scuffle," I replied cautiously. "Would you have any records or perhaps someone handling the deliveries who might know more?"

She sighed, brushing a stray strand of hair behind her ear.

"Albert was our main delivery guy, but since... well, you know... he's obviously not here anymore. As for records, everything's at the main office in the barn. I can check later if you'd like?" She was pretty much telling me she wasn't about to go do it now, and I didn't blame her or think she should drop everything.

I nodded, appreciative of her willingness to help.

"That'd be great, Millard. I'm just trying to connect some dots." I pointed at the pumpkin patch. "Do you mind if I get a few more shots?" I asked.

"Oh course," she said with a playful glint in her eyes. "Always on the hunt for a story, aren't you? I'll see what I can find. In the meantime, enjoy the festivities."

The pumpkin patch didn't provide any of the information I needed to discover if Albert was the target of the double homicide. And I still had to go to Ceramic Celebrations o get photos of the Autumn Art Festival.

As Fern and I walked back toward the lighthouse, our heels clicking against the cobblestone pathway that bordered the seaside, the salty breeze tugged playfully at our hair. The sun was beginning to dip, casting a soft golden glow that turned the waters into a shimmering expanse of gold and blue.

I was preoccupied, mentally cataloging my notes from our visit to the ranch, when Fern grabbed my arm, pulling me to a halt.

"Look," she exclaimed, pointing at a vibrant festival spread out on the beach below us. "The carnival rides have started. I've been wanting to check it out. And you know," she said with a wink, "it might be a great place to scout some potential customers for the pageant school, especially now that Millie Kay has given me the green light."

While the festival did look enticing, I was pressed for time.

"I have to cover the Ceramic Celebration for the journal," I told her, trying to sound apologetic.

"No worries!" Fern replied brightly. "I'll mingle here, and you head on over. We can meet up later."

Feeling a twinge of guilt at leaving Fern behind but knowing I had a responsibility, I continued down the seaside. The sounds of laughter and chatter grew louder as I neared the Ceramic Celebration. The little shops that lined the seafront were adorned with fall-themed decorations, from golden-hued wreaths to bundles of dried corn.

Upon entering the Ceramic Celebration, I was immediately struck by the array of colors. Everywhere I looked, tables were laden with incredible artwork. There were intricate hand-blown glass sculptures that seemed to dance with light, watercolor paintings depicting serene autumn landscapes, and finely crafted ceramic plates painted with detailed scenes of Thanksgiving feasts.

In one corner, children were gathered around tables for the Crafting Workshop. Their small hands were busily creating fall-themed crafts, from leaf-imprinted clay coasters to adorable turkey handprints. The joy on their faces was unmistakable, and the proud parents watched on, cameras in hand.

But what truly captured my attention was a large ceramic centerpiece placed prominently in the middle of the venue. The piece depicted an intricate Thanksgiving scene, with families gathered around a grand table, sharing food and stories. The details were impeccable: the turkey glistened as if freshly roasted, the cranberry sauce gleamed, and the faces of the people were painted with such skill that they seemed alive, laughing and sharing in the celebration.

I approached the artist, and her face lit up with a proud smile as she noticed my interest in her centerpiece. She had a smear of blue paint on her cheek, lending her an endearing charm.

"Hello, I'm Violet from the *Junction Journal*," I told her, extending a hand. "Your work is truly mesmerizing. Would you mind if I interviewed you for tomorrow's morning paper?"

She eagerly shook my hand, and I noticed paint stains of various hues on her fingers. "Of course! I'm Nadia Finch. It's an honor to be featured."

I took out my notepad, ready to jot down her words. "What inspired this incredible Thanksgiving centerpiece?"

"Well, Thanksgiving has always been a special time for my family.

The scene represents my own memories, the warmth and love I've experienced over the years. I wanted to bring that feeling to life." Nadia looked at the ceramic piece fondly.

I snapped a photo of the masterpiece, ensuring I captured its intricate details. Every small plate held a slice of turkey along with the normal Thanksgiving fixings, and the tiny little tiered plates bore realistic-looking desserts—small pies, cupcakes, and even gingerbread cookies. Though they were made of clay, they still looked real enough to eat.

"The details are so precise. How long did it take you to craft this?" I asked.

"Oh, longer than I'd care to admit. Weeks, really. Every character, every dish on the table—each has a story. It's a culmination of many cherished moments." She chuckled softly.

I took a few more photos from different angles, hoping to capture the centerpiece's essence. "Do you have any other pieces here that hold a special meaning to you?"

Nadia led me to a corner in which there rested a smaller ceramic piece, a depiction of children playing in a pile of leaves.

"This one's inspired by my grandchildren. Their joy, their innocence... I wanted to freeze that moment in time," she said in a warm tone.

I smiled, snapping a photo. "It's beautiful. Truly. Your work captures the spirit of fall and Thanksgiving perfectly."

She beamed, clearly touched. "Thank you, Violet. It's heartwarming to know that others can connect with my art. I'd love for you to come up to the art gallery and see me."

"The Winston Art Gallery?" I asked, leaving out just how I knew about it. "In the art district?"

"Yes," she said and put her hand on her chest. "You know the gallery? You like art?"

"I find it fascinating how your mind and other creatives' work. Like that." I pointed at the piece. "I'm not sure I could think of something and then create it."

"Look around." She drew her hands out in front of her. "All these little ones are getting hands-on experience, and that's the best way to learn."

"Do you go to the chamber of commerce meetings here?" I asked.

"I have gone to a handful over the last few weeks. It's hard for everyone in the village to see eye to eye, and I think that's why we stay up in the mountain, but I do love coming down here every so often to help out fellow artists." She smiled. "Why do you ask about the chamber?"

I nodded, taking in Nadia's words.

"I've heard there's been a bit of tension recently about some village matters. Anything you'd like to share?" I asked.

"On or off the record?" Nadia hesitated for a moment, her gaze shifting to a group of children engrossed in painting.

"Off the record," I said, slipping my camera and pad of paper back into the bag.

She took a deep breath.

"Well, I don't like to gossip, but yes, there have been some rather heated discussions at the last few chamber meetings. In particular, Amelia from Sugarbrush Bakery has been quite vocal about wanting to get more organic products up to her shop." She referred to Radley's new girlfriend, someone I had really gotten to know over the last of the summer months.

"She's been making a push for healthier, locally sourced ingredients," I said so it appeared as though I did know something.

"Yes," Nadia continued, "but it seems not everyone sees eye to eye with her. There was a bit of a scuffle at one of the meetings. One of Amelia's employees, a rather assertive young man, got quite confrontational when some vendors seemed reluctant to provide what she was asking for."

My ears perked up at her words.

"Do you know this guy's name?" I asked, fingers crossed in hopes I'd finally get his name.

Nadia shook her head. "No, I don't. But he's hard to miss. Tall, broad-shouldered, always wearing a cap. Seems to be very protective of Amelia and her business interests."

I thought back to the few times I'd been to Sugarbrush Bakery. A guy fitting that description did indeed always seem to be around, handling deliveries, talking to suppliers. But as for his relationship to Amelia, I couldn't say because I'd gone there to see her, not to pay much attention to anything else.

I bit my lip, mulling over this new information. I really liked Amelia and had hoped Radley's budding relationship with her was the real deal. But who was this mysterious man who seemed so invested in her business? And why was he getting into arguments on her behalf?

"Thanks, Nadia," I said, my voice filled with gratitude. "That's some really helpful information."

She smiled warmly. "Always happy to help, Violet. Take care."

I waved goodbye to Nadia and walked out of the Ceramic Celebration, my mind buzzing with questions and possibilities. The more deeply I dug into this investigation, the more intertwined everyone's stories seemed to become.

My phone chirped with a text from Darren, asking me to meet him at the edge of the woods just past the office and beyond a small street of houses.

He'd ended the message by typing, *Hurry up!*

CHAPTER TWELVE

A fter making it to the dead-end street, I took in the scenery and noticed all the cute clapboard houses lining either side of the road had been decorated for fall.

The sound of gentle waves lapping against the beach was behind me. Each cottage home was painted a different vibrant color. Many had boats or motorized water vehicles parked under a car porch, along with a segment of a chain-link fence to divide the properties. All the vehicles were winterized for the season.

My arrival hadn't gone unnoticed. As I passed by the houses, the dogs in the yards barked at me. Most of the houses looked dark, and I could only imagine the residents were all at the seaside getting ready for tonight's festival fireworks and big to-do, since tomorrow the festival activities would be moving more toward Holiday Park.

Holiday Junction was honestly pure charm. Too bad the murders loomed over such a festive time here.

A silhouette stood at the end of the sandy street near the rickety bridge built out of weathered boards. I smiled when I recognized it was Darren, waiting exactly where he wanted me to meet him.

"What took you so long?" Darren asked, back to looking like a disheveled bar owner.

I took a step up on the bridge, taking care not to plant a foot on any of the rusty nails popping out. Clearly, the salty conditions had taken a toll on the boards.

"There is a big festival going on all over town, and there are people to weave in and out of. The big event is on the beach tonight, remember?" I stopped in front of him as he turned his back to the woods.

His eyes grazed the top of my shoulder, and I looked back to see what he'd seen.

"Why so jumpy?" I asked when the only things I noticed were the few seaside cottage houses on the dead-end street. Time was slipping past as the sun was starting to kiss the edge of the ocean.

"We can talk while we go see Vern." He meant Vern McKenna, the wood-carver who made our Merry Maker sign.

"I thought you didn't have time for all that." The sarcasm came spewing out of my mouth. Instantly, I felt bad. "I'm sorry. I know you're working really hard in school, and I admire that. I didn't take into consideration that Diffy Delk is pretty much the only lawyer in Holiday Junction and someone might be using him for legal representation in these murders."

"I'm sorry too." He drew his eyes back to mine and looked down at me. "As soon as I said those things to you, I felt horrible and realized, too, that I have more than just classes to take. I have a life. Responsibilities like the bar and us."

Hearing him say "us" made my heart leap. I'd never truly had a boyfriend before, and I was very grateful I wasn't like most of my friends back in Normal. They were all either married or having babies when I was in my early twenties, and though I was only in my late twenties now, I at least felt like I knew what I wanted in a boyfriend. When Darren acted as such earlier, I'd started to question him.

"I'm so glad you apologized," I said, giving him a pass and a kiss. "Honestly, you don't have to come to see Vern with me. I'm going to have him do..." I started to say my ideas for the final event.

"I called him this morning when you and I talked about the Leaf

Dance event. He already has it cut and painted, ready to go." Darren took my hand, and we hurried down the sandy path.

When the sand of the walkway turned into grass and clay, I knew we were going deeper and deeper into the wooded area of Holiday Junction. Before too long, we could hear Monty, Layla Camsen's dog, barking at the sounds of our footsteps.

"Almost there," I said. I took my phone out of my bag and turned on the flashlight.

Dried branches snapped under our feet, and the shuffling of leaves only made Monty bark more.

In the clearing ahead, the small shedlike structure came into view.

"Monty, hush." Vern stood outside the shed. The light from inside it filtered through the dingy window, casting a glow on the tall, lanky man with thinning hair. "It's just Violet," he said, like Monty understood him.

Maybe he did. He stopped barking as soon as Darren and I walked out of the woods.

"Good evening," Vern said to Darren and me. "How's the case?"

"For now I've only got—" I started to say but stopped when both men looked at me funny. "Oh, you mean Darren."

"Yeah, but it seems like you are looking into it too," Vern said, a smirk on his face as though he knew Darren and I had some sort of tension between us.

He opened the door to the shed, and we were met with the odor of paint. Open spray cans littered the ground. The naked bulb hanging from the ceiling gave off little light. When I scanned up past the paint, I saw a large piece of wood cut out in the form of one large yellow leaf with two smaller orange and red leaves. The latter two leaves conveyed the illusion of dancing or floating down on the edge of the large yellow one.

"It's going." Darren shook his head with a look of disappointment. "There's no real clear reason the Hardens were killed."

"Well, I found a few reasons," I said and ran my hand along the edges of the wooden sign, which would later tonight be placed up in Holiday

Park. There, the Leaf Dance would take place, signaling the Thanksgiving Festival's last hurrah.

"Yeah?" Vern seemed to take a vested interest.

"I'm not sure what all of these people have in common with Albert and Tara for someone to have killed both of them," I said as I began to tell them.

It was a strategic move. I knew Darren couldn't contain his information once I got started, and also Vern had been the Merry Maker years ago and lived in Holiday Junction his whole life. He knew practically everyone, which meant he'd know some if not all of the people I was about to rattle off who could've killed the Hardens.

Darren's eyebrows furrowed in concentration, his usual playfulness momentarily set aside. "Who have you got on your list?"

I took a deep breath, preparing myself. "First, there's Amelia from Sugarbrush Bakery. Radley has been seeing her, and there's this guy who works for her. He got confrontational in a chamber of commerce meeting recently. Amelia's been trying hard to get more organic products for her shop. And Albert's refusal to deliver up to the art district might've been in the way of that."

Vern's eyes narrowed. "Amelia? She's always been a sweet girl. But that fella working for her... I've heard he's a bit of a hothead."

Darren scribbled something in his notebook. "What else?"

"There's also Millard Ramsey," I added. "She's the owner of the Hippity Hoppity Ranch. Someone from the art district had asked if the ranch would deliver up there, but Albert refused."

Darren looked up. "That could be a motive. But it still feels like a stretch that she'd be involved in murder."

Vern nodded. "Millard's a shrewd businesswoman but not violent— not that I've seen, anyway."

"And then there's the art district itself," I ventured. "Nadia from the Ceramic Celebration mentioned the tension at the chamber meetings. She said that not everyone in the village sees eye to eye, implying some divide between the village and the mountain folks."

Darren sighed, looking overwhelmed. "It seems like there are many threads leading to the art district."

Vern scratched his chin thoughtfully. "Albert might've refused delivery up there, but he had friends in that district. You know, this all sounds a bit convoluted."

I nodded. "It is. But somewhere in this web is the truth. We just need to figure out how these pieces fit together."

Darren leaned against the wooden sign. "We've got our work cut out for us. But with all of us putting our heads together, we'll get to the bottom of this."

Vern grinned, breaking the tension. "First things first, let's get this sign up for the Leaf Dance. And then, let the investigation truly begin."

I cocked my head and looked at Vern curiously. "Friends in the art district? That's surprising, considering how Albert seemed to avoid it at all costs, which created a scene at the chamber meeting."

Vern sighed, his face taking on a solemn expression.

"Yes, it's a sad history, really. Albert and Tara didn't always live downtown. They lived up in the art district for years. They were quite involved with the community there," he said, starting a tale.

Darren tilted his head and squinted as if trying to recall it.

Vern nodded slowly. "Aye, they were fixtures up there. Used to host these grand parties and gatherings. But then... tragedy struck." His voice filled with emotion, and he paused. "Their only child, a young boy, was playing outside one day, riding his bike. A tourist, unfamiliar with the winding roads, came speeding around a curve and hit him. The boy didn't survive."

I felt a pang in my heart. "That's heartbreaking," I said.

"No wonder they moved. The pain of such a loss..." Darren looked down, clearly affected by the tragic story.

"They were never the same after that. They left the art district, hoping for a fresh start downtown. But memories like that... They never truly fade. Albert might've had friends up there, but the pain of returning, even just for deliveries, must've been too much." Vern frowned.

A heavy silence enveloped us. A gust of wind rustled the leaves around us, as if nature itself were mourning the sad tale.

After a moment, I finally said, "That puts things in perspective. We need to remember the people behind the headlines, the stories that aren't always told."

"I remember that now that you mention it." Darren nodded.

I hesitated for a moment so the tale could pass and I could move on before we left.

"Did you know about Tara's YouTube channel, Vern? Or has Leni heard anything related to it? She's always got her ear to the ground with village happenings," I joked, although I meant it very seriously. Leni was nosy.

Vern chuckled softly. "Aye, Leni does like to keep informed. Between her tailoring work and being on the Celtic dance team, she meets a lot of folks. And yes, she did mention Tara's channel once or twice. Said it was gaining quite a following."

"Anything specific she's mentioned?" Darren's interest sounded piqued.

"Well, Leni did talk about a luncheon that happened recently," Vern began, rubbing his chin thoughtfully once more. "A gathering of businesswomen from the village. Marianne, Betsy, Cassidy, and Daphne were there."

The calendar had included all those women's names, but it never once referred to Leni.

"Leni said they were all discussing their businesses, upcoming events, and some village gossip, as they often do. She didn't say much about the specifics, but she did mention that Tara's YouTube channel came up."

"And?" Darren pressed.

Vern shrugged. "Leni didn't elaborate too much. Just that there was some talk about the channel's rapid growth and that some folks weren't too pleased about some content Tara was sharing. She felt it might've been digging up memories people would rather forget."

"Like the tragedy of their son?" I furrowed my brow, thinking.

Vern nodded slowly. "It's possible. But Leni said the tone of the conversation shifted quickly, so she didn't get many details. These luncheons tend to be more about networking and less about deep dives."

Darren sighed. "It's another piece of the puzzle, though. We have to consider all angles."

I nodded. "And we should talk to these women, see if they know anything more. Tara's channel might be the key to understanding some of this."

"I guess we've got to get going." Darren decided it was time to leave. "Thanks again for the quick turnaround," he said to Vern about the sign.

We all said goodbye as Darren and I schlepped out into what was now the darkness of the woods, Darren carrying the sign.

"I'll prop it up next to the big oak on the outskirts of the woods, and we can come back later tonight to get it and place it," he said, declaring the plan.

"Sure," I agreed. I wanted so badly to bite my tongue about Marianne Drew, but I couldn't. "I know Marianne is one of your clients, but Darren, we have to talk about her possible involvement."

Darren didn't stop me from talking or try to say anything, so I kept going.

"With the information Vern gave us about the Hardens' son, I have a connection between Marianne and Tara." I chose my words carefully. "Tara and Marianne were planning on doing something for the Mistletoe Masquerade Ball. They'd even toured the Leisure Center, and Mama said Marianne mentioned something about cameras. Then Mama texted me, saying she remembered it was about having Tara go live on her YouTube channel."

The leaves that crunched beneath our feet filled the pauses between my speech. When Darren didn't say anything, I continued with my theory.

"Marianne wanted to move the ball up to the art district this year, and by rights, she can do that, but if she and Tara had something going on with the channel, then Tara could've put the stops on the art district venue because Albert didn't want anything to do with it up there."

I stopped talking when Darren abruptly stopped in front of me. He didn't turn around.

"Just think about it," I said. "Marianne lives for that ball, and it's her life to host it."

He stuck the sign down in the ground and twisted himself around to look at me.

"The ball's primary goal is to raise funds for local charities, particularly those supporting underprivileged children and families during the holiday season." I was rattling off the copy Marianne had already submitted to the *Junction Journal* for an event spotlight. Along with that copy, she'd sent in a sizeable donation.

"Attendees contribute by purchasing high-priced tickets, participating in silent auctions of items donated by local businesses, and making direct donations, which all get donated to the fund and make Marianne look great." I blinked a few times and sucked in a deep breath. "And I got word today from Mayor Paisley's office that Marianne is going to receive the Key to the Village this week at the end of the Thanksgiving Festival. That'll be wherever the Merry Maker places the sign."

Darren stared at me.

"Marianne said the light wasn't good for the show but the natural light at that hour on top of the mountain in the art district would look amazing on it. Tara told her Albert wouldn't go for it, though. Marianne had to get it out of her head. If Marianne's big-time contribution to the village didn't happen and she didn't get that key... You and I both know Marianne is all about her ego." I hated to say it, but I was right, and he knew it.

She was definitely a suspect in my eyes.

"Marianne's ego and status in the community were hurt by Tara's little television show. Marianne had a big ego, so that would have been enough for her to see Albert to try to talk him out of letting Tara host the show. When he didn't agree, a little pushy-push did the trick," I said, telling him what I'd thought earlier. "I'm not saying she meant to kill him, but I am saying Mama had a meeting with Marianne that afternoon. She would've been there."

"I know it doesn't look good, and that's what I wanted to talk to you about," Darren said, his voice breaking. "I wanted to go to law school to help people who are criminally charged for something they didn't do."

The moon was starting to shine through the skeletal branches of the tree, casting a sliver of light on Darren. Though I couldn't see all of his expression, I could see his jaw was tense and his words were hard for him to say.

"Diffy Delk doesn't care if the client committed the crime or not. He said everyone he represents is innocent, and he will treat them as such."

This was not the type of law Darren wanted to practice, and I knew it.

"I can't begin to help Diffy with Marianne's case until I find out for sure that she isn't the killer." He swallowed. Hard. "She told Diffy when I was in the other room that she had gone to see Tara before anyone got to the luncheon."

"She did?" My eyes grew at the thought of her at the scene of at least one murder.

"I remember Millie Kay saying Marianne was coming there, so she might have gone to see Tara first, had an argument with her, and killed her before she came to the Leisure Center. Then she saw Albert and realized what she'd done. Took the opportunity to do like you said, pushy-push. Down he went. Then Millie Kay told you she didn't show up for the appointment—well, it doesn't look good."

"I'm sorry. I know you're going to be an amazing lawyer, but what are you going to do about Diffy?" I asked, changing the subject.

"I'm not going to do anything." The edges of his eyes drooped. He gestured between us. "We are going to find out who killed the Hardens, and I'll use the inside information to do that."

CHAPTER THIRTEEN

I still couldn't forget about the whole Amelia Harman connection. When we made it back to the beach, it was so hard for me to keep quiet until I could decide what to say or do about her employee at the Sugarbrush Bakery, which was in the art district.

I had to know the identity of the man who had gotten into the public fight with Albert. Though Marianne looked more and more like the prime suspect, the fact Albert had had a public fight didn't sit well with me either.

The beach was buzzing with activity. Families gathered around the bonfire, the golden flames casting warm glows on their faces. Children's laughter mingled with the rhythmic sounds of the ocean waves, and in the distance, carnival rides whirred and spun, their vibrant lights illuminating the night sky. The chill of late November nipped at the air, but the anticipation of Thanksgiving warmed everyone's spirits.

Well, it warmed the spirits of those who didn't know about the double homicide.

Darren and I quickly spotted Radley's tall figure. He was chatting animatedly with Amelia Hartman, owner of Sugarbrush Bakery and someone I needed to talk to. But was tonight the time to have that conversation?

Her lively red curls caught the fire's light, dancing as if they had a life of their own. The retro-inspired outfit she wore, patterned with all sorts of colors, caught my eye once more, reminding me of the artistry that Amelia brought to her craft.

"Violet! Darren!" Amelia greeted us with a wide grin, her eyes twinkling with that familiar mischief. "You made it! I was just telling Radley about my latest creation for the bakery."

"We wouldn't miss it," Darren replied.

I gave Amelia a warm hug.

"It's always good to see you, Amelia." I looked at the situation, trying to gauge if now was a good time to ask about her employee. "Tell us about your creation."

Amelia's eyes lit up, her passion evident as she began to describe her newest work of art.

"All right, so I've been experimenting for weeks to come up with something that truly encapsulates the essence of Thanksgiving, and I think I've finally nailed it," she said so quickly, excitement lacing her voice.

"Imagine a three-tiered pie but not just any pie. The bottom layer is a deep, rich pecan pie with caramelized pecans and a hint of bourbon for that extra warmth. The middle layer is a classic pumpkin pie but with a twist. I've infused it with a hint of orange zest and a touch of cardamom to elevate the traditional flavors. And the top tier? A light, airy cranberry mousse pie with a sprinkle of candied orange peel for a bit of zest." She took a deep breath, and now her excitement was contagious.

I couldn't help but let out an appreciative whistle, my mouth watering at the mere description.

"That sounds incredible, Amelia," I said.

"But wait, there's more," she said with a wink. "The entire masterpiece is encased in a buttery, flaky pie crust that's been brushed with cinnamon-infused honey. And to top it all off, there's a decorative lattice with intertwined leaves and turkeys made of pie dough, giving it a festive look."

"That's not just a dessert, Amelia. That's an entire Thanksgiving experience in one bite," Darren said with a grin.

"I wanted to create something that truly honored the spirit of Thanksgiving—a blend of traditions, flavors, and memories all in one dish." Amelia smiled, her cheeks rosy from the fire and her pride.

Radley clapped her on the back. "Leave it to you to take pies to the next level. I can't wait to try it."

"You'll have to wait," Amelia promised. "I'm unveiling it at our special Friendsgiving."

We all sat around a bonfire that had enough seats for the four of us. Amelia was busy talking to Darren, who knew to keep her occupied so I could talk to Radley.

"Anything at the art district?" I asked, taking the opportunity Darren had afforded me.

Radley cleared his throat, glancing around as if ensuring we weren't overheard.

"I managed to make contact with Cassidy during the Cook-Off Contest. She called Tara this morning. Said she couldn't make it to any meetings because of a house showing," he said.

I raised an eyebrow, signaling my surprise that she had an alibi.

"Yes, and with Christmas approaching, she's swamped. Apparently, she's trying to make as much as she can for presents and her contribution to the Mistletoe Masquerade Ball." Radley looked thoughtful. "So, in short, she's off the suspect list."

"That's one less person to consider," I said.

I nodded, my gaze drifting across the beach. Holiday Junction's atmosphere was electric, with the festive season approaching and the underlying tension of the ongoing investigation.

"We should continue to narrow down our list," I said, turning back to Radley. "The more we know, the closer we get to the truth."

"Yeah. Do you want to meet up in the morning and go over who we have left?" Radley asked. "I'll be in there early to download all the photos I took up there for the cook-off and the art gallery."

That was a sure sign that he didn't want to talk about it and would rather enjoy Amelia's company. He wanted to have fun on his night off now that he'd done the reporting required of him.

"Yes. We can also divvy up tomorrow's events so we can get them all in," I said, deciding to let it go and just enjoy the time I had here with friends.

CHAPTER FOURTEEN

The chill of the early morning wrapped around me as I stepped out of my garage apartment. Even though the sun had yet to rise, the sky was painted in a delicate dance of blush pink and lavender, hinting at the promise of a gorgeous fall day.

The first thing that struck me was the smell. It was that unmistakable crispness of fall, when the air had just a hint of woodsmoke and drying leaves. That scent always reminded me of turning a book's pages, a fresh chapter in the story of the year.

I walked toward the outdoor living area between my garage and my parents' house and noticed the flickering flames in their outdoor fireplace dancing merrily and sending sparks up into the fading early morning. The soft crackling sound reached my ears before I even noticed my daddy sitting on the couch.

Dad was wrapped in a thick flannel robe, his hands cradling a steaming mug of coffee. The gentle flame illuminated his face, highlighting the laugh lines and wisdom that came with years.

"Early bird," he greeted, his voice rich and deep, softened by the morning tranquility.

"Just trying to get ahead," I replied, pulling my jacket more tightly around me. "What about you?"

The outdoor couch looked so inviting. Its plush cushions were piled high with soft blankets, forming the sort of place you could easily sink into and lose hours.

"Ah, couldn't sleep. Your mama is tossing and turning from the events of yesterday." The orange light from the fireplace reflected off the screen of the iPad Dad held up. "Read the online edition of the *Junction Journal*, Vi? Your piece is up."

I hesitated, the information I'd gathered from yesterday's conversations and the importance of the story pressing on me. "Not yet. Wanted to make sure it uploaded correctly from my laptop. How does it look?"

He tilted the screen toward me, an invitation to come closer. I walked over, the warmth of the fire welcoming me as I sat beside him on the couch. The comfort of the cushions and the heat from the fireplace made it tempting to stay longer than I intended.

Dad leaned over to the small table beside the couch, where a pot of freshly brewed coffee sat. It was one of his morning rituals—a pot of strong, black coffee waiting for the early risers. He poured a cup, and the steam curled up, carrying the rich aroma of ground beans. Without asking, he added a splash of cream, just the way I liked it, and handed me the steaming mug.

"Grab a coaster before you sit down." He gestured to the table. "You know your mama and coasters," he said as if it were a joke, but it was definitely not.

Nor was Mama's seriousness about decorating anything she owned, including the outdoor space of the home she shared with Dad.

The outdoor table was one of Mama's masterpieces. Millie Kay never did things by halves. The long, family-style table was a riot of autumnal colors. It was as if she'd managed to capture the essence of fall and lay it out for all to see. Pumpkins of every size and shade sat nestled amongst twisted gourds, their unique shapes and patterns providing a visual feast. Scattered among the fruits were leaves in deep reds, oranges, and yellows, each one picked for its perfection. It was a tableau of fall, a still life painting made real.

I took a coaster, set it on the small table in front of the couch, and then took the cup Dad had poured for me.

"Thanks, Dad," I murmured, wrapping my hands around the cup and letting the warmth seep into my fingers as I sat down next to him.

He just nodded, scanning the screen before him. A comfort resided in the silence between us, a mutual understanding that sometimes, words weren't necessary.

Unlike my relationship with Mama, whose lips were always flapping. Silence was not appropriate when she was around.

I took a deep breath and began to read. My words, juxtaposed against images from the crime scene and photos of the Hardens, painted a vivid picture of the events that had transpired. Every sentence, every paragraph was carefully crafted, balancing the need for truth with the respect for those involved.

Double Homicide Rocks Holiday Junction: A Beloved Couple Found Dead

By Violet Rhinehammer, Editor in Chief

HOLIDAY JUNCTION – *In a shocking turn of events that has left the community in disbelief, a prominent local couple, Albert and Tara Harden, were tragically found dead yesterday.*

Albert Harden was discovered at the Leisure Center, a hub for local events and gatherings. The exact circumstances surrounding his death are still under investigation. Meanwhile, Tara Harden was found deceased in the pair's family residence on Candy Stripe Avenue.

The Hardens, known for their generous philanthropic activities and active involvement in community events, were deeply cherished members of Holiday Junction. Their unexpected demise has left gaping holes in the hearts of many, with tributes pouring in from all corners of the village.

Police Chief Matthew Strickland, who is heading the investigation, has urged anyone with any information related to these incidents to come forward. "We understand the pain and shock that our community is experiencing. We are working diligently to get to the bottom of this," Strickland said in an official statement.

The investigation is still in its early stages, and law enforcement officials have refrained from speculating about any potential motives or suspects for now. They've also emphasized the importance of accurate information to ensure that justice is served.

Residents and local businesses are urged to assist in any way possible. If you have any relevant information or noticed any suspicious activity in the vicinity of the Leisure Center or the Harden residence, please contact Police Chief Matthew Strickland at (123) 456-7890.

As we mourn the loss of Albert and Tara, let's come together as a village to help ensure that the truth is uncovered and justice prevails.

"You've done well, Vi," Dad finally broke the silence, his voice filled with pride. "It's a delicate subject, but you've approached it with grace and professionalism."

I took a sip of my coffee, and the rich flavors grounded me. "Thanks, Dad. It wasn't easy, especially with how close it hits to home. But the community needs to know."

He reached over, placing a comforting hand on my shoulder.

"That's the weight of the pen, or in this case, the keyboard. But remember, you're giving a voice to the story, to the truth. And that's important," he said in a way that told me he'd handle Mama if she got her panties in a wad.

Our eyes met, and in that moment, I felt an overwhelming gratitude for this man, for these quiet moments shared in the glow of the morning light. Whatever challenges the day brought, with family and truth on my side, I felt ready to face them.

"Time to face the music," I said and took another sip of the coffee. "Do you think she'll recognize if I take this mug to go?"

"Not if you bring it back in one piece, clean, and set it right back where you got it." He smirked, since he knew Mama all too well.

"I can do that." I put the mug on the table and gave him a hug before I picked up my bag. Then I stood and slung the bag over my shoulder. "A reporter's job is never done."

Dad filled up the mug for me to take, and I was off.

My mind was reeling with so many things on my way to the office that instead of trying to catch the trolley, I wanted to walk. I could let the tangled web of information try to untangle itself as the fresh, brisk early morning air seeped into my brain with the help of the coffee.

I wanted to get into the office early so I could write down all the clues on the board and divvy up the day's festival activities, which would take place at Holiday Park, between Radley and me.

I walked down Heart Way and took a left on Main Street before I took a right going toward Holiday Park. It was easiest to walk the path down to the seaside at this hour instead of waiting for Goldie's trolley to come pick me up.

The soft glow of the lanterns lighting the paths of Holiday Park began to come into view. The stillness of the predawn hour was broken only by the chirping of a few early birds and the soft rustling of the leaves. The Thanksgiving Festival had transformed our park into a cornucopia of festivities. I could see the outlines of booths being set up for the pie-eating contest and the turkey trot race later in the day. Near the boating dock, a long wooden platform had been established for the log-rolling competition, a playful nod to our town's logging history.

The aroma of cinnamon and cloves wafted through the air as some dedicated vendor was already preparing hot cider to serve throughout the day. The amphitheater stood at one end of the park for local musicians to play their sets, and I remembered talk of a square dance happening tonight. Nearby, children would engage in workshop for making corn husk dolls, recreating a beloved pastime of our ancestors.

I was deep in thought, imagining the laughter and joy the day would bring, when the Merry Maker sign suddenly caught my attention.

Its majestic silhouette stood tall between the shimmering lake and the iconic Holiday Fountain, illuminated only by the park's soft lighting.

My heart swelled with pride. That sign meant so much more than just a marker; it was the culmination of history, tradition, and community spirit.

But as I thought about how I would write an article on the sentiment of the Leaf Dance and its significance, a glint of something in my peripheral vision caught my attention. I instinctively reached for my camera, thinking of capturing the sign in its mystique at the current hour.

But as I adjusted the lens, a sharp pain surged through my head.

The world began to blur and spin uncontrollably. The last image my mind registered was that of a brick lying nearby, hints of white smeared along its side. Darkness began to consume my vision, and with one last desperate attempt to call for help, I succumbed to unconsciousness.

CHAPTER FIFTEEN

The soft and rhythmic sensation of something wet on my cheek slowly dragged me back to consciousness.

My eyes fluttered open, and the sight of Mayor Paisley's concerned little eyes and black-and-white fur came into focus. The Boston terrier was vigorously licking my face, a clear sign of distress in his demeanor. Through my daze, I could hear Kristine Whitlock, his owner, frantically speaking into her phone, no doubt calling for help.

"I was walking the mayor, and I found her in the park. She's breathing," I heard her say. "Wait. Her eyes are open."

"Hurry, please," Kristine continued, her voice shaking slightly. "She's got a bump on her head, and she's clutching a brick. There's blood... There's a broken coffee mug. I think she was attacked. We're by the Holiday Fountain in the park, next to the Merry Maker sign."

She paused for a moment, listening to the dispatcher's response. "Yes, it's Violet. Violet Rhinehammer. She's disoriented. Please, send someone quickly."

Mayor Paisley whined, echoing Kristine's concerns.

"I'll stay with her until help arrives," she said. "Just please hurry."

Panic welled up in me as I tried to recall what had happened. My fingers found the brick I had clutched, and I felt a sticky residue on its surface.

"You're going to be okay." Kristine stood over me and looked the way my insides felt.

Mayor Paisley had moved from licking my face to licking the brick.

"Don't do that," Kristine scoffed at her and tugged her leash back. "I'm so sorry, Violet. I can't believe this."

My mind couldn't formulate the words I wanted to say, so I just lay there listening as the ambulance's wailing siren grew louder, and soon enough, I felt myself being loaded onto a stretcher.

The ride was a blur, but the next thing I knew, I was inside the village clinic—a small but cozy wooden cabin nestled amongst towering pines and mountain vistas. Its interior, made of polished timber, gave off a comforting warmth. Through the window, the imposing beauty of the mountains near the art district loomed large. The sheer majesty of the scene momentarily relieved the pain throbbing in my head.

I'd never been here, so it was nice to try to look around and take my mind off the fact that my mouth wasn't working.

Mama entered the room with a concerned expression, her eyes glistening with tears. Dad, Darren, and Chief Strickland followed closely behind, all wearing faces etched with worry. The patient room was small, but it felt crowded with love and concern.

As I attempted to sit up, I felt the room sway a little.

Darren rushed to my side and gently urged me to lie back down.

I glanced at the brick still clutched in my hand, and curious, I brought it closer to my face. There, caked onto its rough surface, was a familiar white substance. The sugary scent immediately registered in my brain—it was frosting.

"Frosting?" I whispered, more to myself than anyone else.

"What did she say?" Mama asked the doctor, who had sped over to me. He took his little flashlight and shined it from eye to eye, blinding me.

"Ahem." I found the strength to clear my throat and brought my bloody hand up to my face.

"Mama, I broke your mug," I knew the blood came from me falling with the mug in my hand and getting cut.

Mama laughed.

"Don't you worry about any old stinking mug," she said as the stress started to melt from her face.

I glanced around her at my dad. He was smiling, knowing the conversation we'd had about Mama and her mug. He winked at me.

Chief Strickland approached the bed.

"Seems like our attacker wanted to send a specific message." He held out an evidence bag.

I held the brick up to give it to him, but I pulled it back when I saw the white stuff in the brick holes, remembering that Mayor Paisley had licked it.

Instead of dropping it in the evidence bag, I brought the brick up to my nose and instantly knew the smell.

Frosting.

My mind raced, trying to piece together the events. How did frosting end up on a brick meant to hurt me?

Sugarbrush Bakery. Amelia's employee.

"I'm sorry. I need the brick for evidence," Chief Strickland said as I continued clutching it. "We can't have people going around throwing bricks, Violet," he said, talking to me like I was a child.

I nodded weakly and relinquished my hold on the brick, feeling a twinge of pain at the sudden movement. As Chief Strickland slid the brick into an evidence bag, I could hear muffled voices outside the room.

"...clear signs of a concussion," Dr. Lansing said in a calm voice that floated through the fabric barrier. "She's lucky. It could've been much worse."

"Can she come home with us, Doctor?" Mama's voice trembled slightly.

"Yes, she can go home. But she needs complete rest over the Thanksgiving break," Dr. Lansing replied. "She might experience dizziness, blurred vision, or trouble with memory. It's essential she doesn't strain herself. Let her rest, keep her surroundings calm, and return to see me next week for a follow-up."

"We'll make sure she's comfortable and looked after," Dad added in his own reassuring voice.

"I don't like the idea of her being alone. What if whoever did this comes back?" Darren piped up, concern evident.

"We'll keep an eye out," Chief Strickland replied gruffly. "We have a couple of officers who can patrol Heart Way."

I wanted to speak, to assure them I was okay, to dive deeply into the mystery of why someone would target me. But exhaustion laid heavily on my limbs and clouded my thoughts.

I heard the footsteps of my family and friends as they came back into the room, where I saw their concerned faces.

"All right, Violet. You're free to go," Dr. Lansing said with a gentle smile, patting my arm reassuringly. "Remember what I said. Rest up, and we'll see you next week."

The brisk morning air felt sharp against my face, but it was invigorating.

My family hovered around me, clearly worried, but I was determined.

"Rest, my hiney!" I exclaimed with feigned exasperation, my Southern roots showing. "I'm fine, y'all. Just a little bump on the head."

"Violet, you can't possibly think of going to the office right now," Mama said, her voice edged with anxiety.

"Actually, Mama, that's exactly what I'm thinking," I replied defiantly.

"You're as stubborn as a mule," Dad muttered, but I saw the hint of a smile tugging at the corners of his mouth.

"Darren, back me up here, son," Chief Strickland said, trying to use my close friend as a voice of reason.

But Darren, reading the determined look in my eyes, just sighed.

"She's made up her mind. How about I offer her a ride? That way, she isn't walking all alone." Darren gestured to his moped. Two helmets were attached to the back of it.

Everyone seemed to weigh the options, and though no one was thrilled, they all relented.

Climbing onto the back of Darren's moped with a helmet strapped on my sore head, I wrapped my arms around him, feeling the steady hum of the machine beneath us.

We weaved our way through the streets of Holiday Junction as the town came alive. I couldn't help but feel the bandage around my hand.

When Darren pulled up outside Brewing Beans, the aroma of fresh coffee beckoned.

"Wait here," Darren said, putting the stand on his moped. "I'll get your coffee. Anything special today?"

"Just a black," I called out as my attention diverted.

Across the street, the charming facade of Flowerworks beckoned, its vibrant flowers in full display. And there stood Betsy Carmichael, arranging a fresh bouquet.

I made my decision in an instant, darting across the street to meet her. This was my chance to have a word with one of the last people to see Tara. My reporter instincts kicked in, pushing past the throbbing pain in my head. Whatever had happened at Tara's house, Betsy would have a clue, and I was determined to find it.

As I approached Flowerworks, the fullness of its beauty was even more stunning up close. Cascades of golden sunflowers framed the entrance, their dark centers gazing up at the morning sun. Ivy draped delicately over the door, intertwined with strings of twinkling fairy lights.

A large wooden barrel stood next to the entrance, overflowing with chrysanthemums in shades of maroon, deep oranges, and golds, reflecting the colors of fall. Nearby, a table was set with smaller vases, each containing a single rose that shimmered in hues of lavender, peach, and ruby red. Their fragrance, a blend of sweet and earthy notes, wafted in the air.

When I walked in, Betsy had already gone to stand near a white-washed counter, her hands dancing skillfully over a bouquet of lilies, dahlias, and wildflowers. The combination was a symphony of colors— purples, pinks, yellows, and blues. Every flower testified to her expertise and the love she poured into her craft.

Her fingers worked nimbly, adding a sprig of baby's breath here, a fern frond there, turning the already breathtaking arrangement into a masterpiece. It wasn't hard to see why Tara had chosen Flowerworks for her gatherings; the blooms spoke of passion, beauty, and a touch of mystery.

"Violet! What brings you here so early?" Betsy's voice broke through my trance, her surprised eyes meeting mine before she noticed the bandage on my hand.

I tried to maintain a casual tone, despite the urgency I felt. "Morning, Betsy. Just thought I'd take in some beauty before heading to work. And, well, I had a few questions I hoped you could help with."

She paused for a moment, her fingers still among the petals, and then nodded, signaling for me to continue. The news of recent events hung in the air between us, but beneath the canopy of colorful blossoms, I hoped to find the truth.

"What happened to your hand?" she asked, fiddling with the stems as if she were trying to change the subject. She seemed like she already knew I would ask her about her running off from Tara's house yesterday morning, when she noticed something had gone awfully wrong before her arrival.

Betsy hesitated. Her eyes darted around the flower-laden room before settling back on mine. "When I saw the commotion at Tara's place, I had a sinking feeling something was terribly wrong. I'd come by to bring her the flowers"—she motioned to similar arrangements on a nearby counter—"and when I saw the police cars, my heart dropped."

I frowned, recalling the moment. "I did notice you among the gathered crowd outside her house. You looked quite shaken and left pretty quickly. What did you see or hear?"

"Honestly, Violet, I didn't see much. I was coming to deliver the flowers for our luncheon. When I approached her house and saw the crowd, the police cars... and you standing there looking devastated, I just knew. I felt this tightness in my chest and panicked. It didn't feel right to be there with flowers in hand, not under those circumstances. It just felt..." She sighed, visibly pained.

Nodding slowly, I continued, "On Tara's calendar, I noticed your name along with Daphne Marsh, Cassidy, and Marianne Drew. Were all of you supposed to meet her yesterday?"

Betsy nodded, her fingers absently stroking a delicate petal.

"Yes. Tara had planned a little get-together. I was supposed to supply the flowers, of course. But now..." She trailed off, her voice heavy with sadness.

"It's all right, Betsy," I offered gently. "I'm just trying to piece together everything. Any detail could be crucial."

She met my gaze squarely, her eyes glistening.

"I wish I could tell you more. I wish I had stayed longer, spoken to someone, but I was so scared, and everything felt so surreal." She frowned.

I nodded, understanding her shock.

"Thank you for sharing that with me. Every little bit helps, and I hope we can get to the bottom of this soon," I said. Then I decided to move into deeper questions about the other intended guests.

Gathering my thoughts, I looked intently at Betsy, searching her eyes for any sign of the answers I was seeking.

"Betsy," I began, the gravity of my next question evident in my tone, "do you have any idea if either Daphne Marsh or Marianne Drew had any motives to... you know, harm the Hardens?"

Betsy looked taken aback, her lips parting slightly in surprise.

"Oh, Violet! That's a serious accusation. I... I don't like to gossip, but since this is a matter of a criminal investigation..." She seemed so put off.

Then she hesitated, her fingers nervously toying with the edge of a tablecloth.

"Well, Daphne and Tara had been at odds lately. It was no secret. They had a falling-out over some committee decisions for the land next to the Leisure Center. But I can't imagine it escalating to... this." She shook her head. "Grief does things to people in different ways."

"Grief?" I asked.

"Tara and Albert's son was killed by a car." Betsy went on to retell the story I'd already heard from Vern. This was the second time I'd heard it, so in my investigative mind, I knew this was something I should probably look into. "But his body wasn't where the accident was. In fact"—she gulped—"the person who hit him actually took his body and buried it in the lot next to the Leisure Center."

Tears welled in my eyes as my heart sank.

"I had no idea." I gasped, wondering why Vern had left that little detail out of his story.

"Yeah, and well, Daphne wants the land developed and is in talks with Cassidy to see what investors they could sell the land to, since Daphne does own it." Betsy blinked. "All of us have been friends for a long time and supported the Hardens, but it's time to move on. Albert was on the board for development, and he kept shooting the vote down every time the idea of Daphne getting a permit to have the land developed was brought up . We all asked Tara if we could come over for lunch to discuss the Mistletoe Masquerade Ball, when in reality, we were going to talk to her about the land and how we could help her move on."

"And Marianne?" I prompted.

Betsy took a deep breath. "Marianne... She and Tara had the YouTube thing going. Recently, there were some rumors that Marianne had given Tara a recipe for the show and that recipe was stolen from…" She stopped talking. "From Amelia at the Sugarbrush Bakery."

I mulled over her words, absorbing the implications. Motives were often more complex than they appeared on the surface.

My mind raced, trying to piece together the puzzle. The connections linking the land, the tragic loss of the Hardens' son, and the simmering tensions within the community were intricate.

"The Sugarbrush Bakery? So you're saying that there might have been a feud between Tara and Amelia over a stolen recipe? And Marianne was in the middle of it?" I asked, trying to clarify the web of information Betsy had shared.

She nodded, her face growing paler. "Yes. Tara was quite upset when she found out that the recipe Marianne shared with her was actually Amelia's. She felt betrayed. She believed Marianne had gone behind her back to sabotage the show because it was gaining popularity. Things have been tense between them since."

"If that's the case, why was Marianne trying to incorporate her into using the Leisure Center for the upcoming Mistletoe Masquerade Ball Marianne puts on every year?" I asked.

"Marianne has already planned for the ball to be in the art district. She only made the appointment with Millie Kay so Tara would think the ball was going to remain down here in the village. Tara and Albert didn't want anything to do with the art district, and we just can't grow as a community if we don't start incorporating all of the village."

Something Betsy said caught my attention.

"Are you saying the art district and the village here split after the Hardens' son passed?" Suddenly, it had become obvious.

"Yes." She looked down, shame on her face. "I hate to say it, but all of us who had shops and lived in the village decided to just cut the art district off."

"Why? It wasn't their fault up there about the son," I said.

"Oh yes it was." She nodded emphatically. "After what happened to Tara's son, we went to the district to have them put street signs up around all the curves, but they refused, saying the signs didn't 'go with the vibe.'" She jerked her head and mocked how the art district's residents talked. "They said that according to the investigation into the death, the boy was in the middle of the road on his bike when he was hit by a tourist who drove their car around the corner. If he'd been on the side of the road like the law states, he wouldn't have been hit. It still didn't make it better that the driver had taken their son's body and buried it down here."

Betsy's eyes clouded with pain. Evidently, this topic wasn't one she often discussed. "The driver... What ever became of him?" I asked gently.

She took a deep breath, her fingers fidgeting with a silk ribbon from one of the flower arrangements.

"He's in prison. Not just for hitting the boy—accidents can, unfortunately, happen. But it was what he did afterward. Hiding the body... It's just unfathomable." She shuddered, visibly upset by the memory.

"The act of hiding the body—that's what made it so much worse. It went from an accident to something sinister." I nodded in understanding.

"Exactly. The burying of the body—that was what really sealed his fate. The community couldn't forgive that. No matter what argument he or his lawyer made, there's just no excuse for that kind of inhumanity." She wiped a tear from her eye.

Then she paused, collecting herself.

"He's serving a long sentence. They labeled it manslaughter due to negligence, and then there was the act of burying the body—a clear attempt to evade responsibility. The court had no mercy on him," she noted.

The gravity of the situation settled upon us. A tragic accident that led to even more heartbreaking choices and an entire community torn apart in its wake.

"Now I can only believe Tara and Albert are at peace..." She trailed off.

I took a moment to gather my thoughts, considering how to approach such a delicate question.

Finally, looking Betsy straight in the eyes, I inquired, "Betsy, with all that you know and the tensions in the village, who do you think might have killed the Hardens?"

Betsy seemed startled by the directness of the question. She took a moment, glancing around her shop as if the flowers might hold the answer.

"Oh, Violet." She sighed. "That question's been haunting me since I heard the news. I've known most folks in this village for years, and it's hard to believe anyone here could commit such an act."

She paused and looked thoughtful.

"But given the recent disputes over the land, the tensions with the art district, and the old wounds regarding Tara's son, there are unfortunately a few people who might have had motive. But I don't want to point fingers without any concrete evidence."

"Of course, I understand. But it helps to know where to look and what pieces of the puzzle might be missing." I was really hoping she'd tell me anything, but I could see her lips were pretty tight.

CHAPTER SIXTEEN

The information of the morning pressed heavily on me as I stepped into the familiar confines of the *Junction Journal* office.

"Violet, you're here? You should be at home resting!" Radley was shocked after seeing me walk through his office's entrance.

I shook my head, feeling a small twinge of pain but ignoring it.

"We've hit a nerve, Radley. Someone doesn't want me to figure out what happened to the Hardens, and I'm not going to let them scare me off," I said, determined now.

"You're something else, you know that? But please, be careful." He looked at me, admiration and concern in his eyes.

Without wasting a moment, I moved to my office. My murder board loomed ahead, an organized chaos of photos, notes, and strings connecting dots. But now, there was so much more to add.

Before I started to add what I'd learned this morning, I saw that Radley had added the information he'd gathered from seeing Cassidy last night.

I began scribbling on the board, detailing everything Betsy had told me.

The rift between the village and the art district, the tragic death of the Hardens' son, Marianne's YouTube feud, and most importantly, the new information about the land next to the Leisure Center. As I pinned the note up, I couldn't help but think how deeply entwined the Hardens' past was with those of so many people in the village.

Next, I added a note about the mysterious frosted brick. It was a bold message, one that led directly to Amelia and the Sugarbrush Bakery.

But why would she want to hurt me? Was it a warning, or was it a threat?

I stepped back, taking in the entirety of the board.

Radley appeared at the door, watching me. He approached the board and scanned the meticulous details I'd pinned up. "You've been busy," he noted with a half smile, though his eyes indicated a more somber understanding of the implications.

"That's one way to put it," I replied with a heavy sigh. "Everything seems to circle back to the rift between the village and the art district."

He pointed at the note about the Hardens' son.

"That's heartbreaking. It's no wonder there's so much tension. But the link to the Leisure Center land and the Mistletoe Masquerade Ball... It's convoluted." He paused, frowning. "And then this thing with the recipe? It's a mess."

"It is," I agreed. "But I think if I can get to the art district and dig around a little, I might be able to untangle some of this mess."

Radley leaned against my desk.

"Before you go, let's look at the Holiday Park events. Might give us some more insight or at least a timeline to work with," he said.

I leaned back in my chair, scanning the various notes pinned to the murder board. Seeing all the information in one place was a visual overload, but it was necessary to keep everything straight before I moved to the whiteboard that listed the events for the festival today.

"We have the pie-eating contest, the Turkey Trot race, and the log-rolling competition," I said.

"I think we should make an appearance at the festival events. The turkey trot race always brings in a good crowd. Could be a good place to hear some chatter." He glanced at my hand then said, "I think whoever did that to you will be keeping an eye out to see if they did stop you, so being at the park will send a clear message that you aren't scared."

I smirked. "True."

With all of our equipment gathered and notebooks in hand, Radley and I decided to walk to Holiday Park. Walking there was a great way to clear my now-throbbing head and get some fresh air.

Also, we stopped by the caramel apple stand. I got an apple rolled in nuts, and Radley opted for the sliced apples with caramel on top.

When we got to the lake, the logging competition was underway.

I got my camera out and started to take photos, while Radley went ahead to the Turkey Trot route to catch runners in action.

The air by the lake was filled with excitement, laughter, and the distant sounds of spirited cheering. The sun reflected off the water, creating a mesmerizing dance of shimmering light that set a picturesque backdrop for the log-rolling competition.

Children lined the edges of the dock, their faces canvases of anticipation with eyes wide as saucers, waiting for the next contestant to take their chance on the slippery logs.

I carefully positioned myself at an angle that allowed me to capture both the competitors and the crowd's reactions through the lens of my camera. Sometimes the images said more than the article, and I really wanted to capture the essence of the participants' and spectators' happy faces, since I'd published the Harden article this morning.

The lake's edge was lined with spectators, some seated on blankets, others on foldable chairs, all eagerly watching the ongoing competition.

A whistle blew, and two new competitors hopped onto their respective logs. Their feet moved quickly in the contestants' attempts to find a rhythm and balance on the wet, rotating wood. Splashes of water hit my lens as their feet occasionally slipped, sending droplets flying.

The scene was an intricate dance of agility, wit, and sheer determination. Some rollers tried to disrupt their opponents by changing the log's pace or splashing water toward them, eliciting playful boos from the audience.

A particularly spirited duo caught my attention. Their fierce yet friendly rivalry was evident. They grinned at each other, exchanged banter, and made exaggerated gestures that had the crowd in tears from laughing so hard.

One tried a daring move, hopping into the air before landing back on the log, but his misjudgment sent him crashing into the water with a spectacular splash. The crowd roared with laughter again, and even his opponent couldn't help but chuckle as he offered a hand to help him back up.

Moving through the crowd, I chatted with a few of the spectators, getting their thoughts on the competition and jotting down notes.

A little girl with braided hair tugged at my sleeve and pointed at the log rollers. "It's like they're dancing on water," she said, her voice filled with wonder.

I had to agree with her. The competition was not just about athleticism; it was a dance, a performance that captured the heart and spirit of our community's tradition. The cheerful atmosphere, the camaraderie among competitors, and the shared joy of the spectators reminded me of why I loved my job.

It was moments like these, when I could step back and capture the essence of a community coming together, that truly made my work feel like a privilege. I briefly forgot what I had to do next when I heard the clink of the trolley bell as the vehicle came into full view.

Goldie was at the wheel and letting people off as I approached.

Seeing Goldie was always a delight, especially today, since she wore her festive getup. She looked every bit the spirited resident of our town, embracing every occasion with a touch of whimsy.

"Goldie!" I called out, waving and making my way toward her as the last of the passengers disembarked from the trolley.

Her eyes crinkled into a familiar smile as she spotted me, but her expression quickly turned into a frown as she took in my condition. "Oh, Violet, dear!" she exclaimed. "Heard about what happened to you. Are you sure you should be out and about?"

I chuckled lightly, trying to wave off her concern. "I'm fine, Goldie.

Just a little shaken, but I won't let that stop me from getting to the bottom of this."

Goldie's festive turkey earrings dangled as she shook her head, clicking her tongue. "You're a tougher cookie than I had anticipated you were going to be when I first met you. But maybe, just maybe, you should be resting up at home, putting your feet up. I've got a good mind to drive you there myself."

"Actually," I began, giving her my best persuasive smile, "I was hoping you could give me a lift to the art district. There are some things I need to follow up on."

Goldie eyed me suspiciously, the turkey on her hat seeming to scrutinize me too.

"You sure you're up for it? The art district is bustling this time of the year, especially today," she said, looking at me from the big mirror above her head as I took a seat behind her.

"I'm sure. It's important." I nodded determinedly. "Sugarbrush Bakery."

She sighed, and her warm gaze softened.

"All right, but on one condition. You promise me if you feel any bit of unease or dizziness, you'll come right back. And if anyone gives you trouble, you call me," she made me promise.

"Deal." I chuckled, touched by her protective streak.

With that, she slammed the trolley door shut and stepped on the gas, guiding the trolley along the roundabout before hitting the curvy road from downtown to the village's art district.

Navigating the art district's enchanting lanes, I was instantly drawn into its mesmerizing realm, just like I had been every time I'd come up since the summer. Every corner felt like a page from a storybook, alive with color, energy, and imagination.

The district took on a different feel now that it was autumn rather than summer.

The streets were dotted with quaint stores, each exuding its own distinctive charm. Lush bouquets overflowed from florists' shops, permeating the air with their intoxicating aroma. Artistic boutiques showcased handcrafted wonders in window displays, tempting onlookers to venture inside.

A rich tapestry of architectural designs adorned the district. There were age-old structures with Victorian elegance, boasting detailed balconies and decorative wrought iron. Interspersed among them were contemporary buildings, their sleek designs framed by expansive glass panels. Vines and ivy romantically draped themselves over the brickwork, adding a dash of nature's artistry.

The sidewalks bustled with life. I spotted artists, lost in their creative worlds, sketching or painting scenes from the vibrant streetscape. Locals and visitors alike ambled leisurely, drawn in by the myriad treasures on offer. The people's cheerful exchanges and bubbling laughter added a soundtrack to this animated setting.

Sunbeams pierced through the leafy cover overhead, creating a playful dance of light and shadow on the pathways. Everywhere I looked, bursts of floral hues from window boxes and suspended pots enlivened the panorama. In this artistic enclave, past and present seemed to embrace, bound together by a shared passion for beauty.

The trolley's gentle hum accompanied my thoughts as we drifted more deeply into the district going toward Sugarbrush Bakery.

"Here ya go," Goldie said, opening the trolley doors. "Don't forget you promised if you're feeling bad, you're going to call."

"I promise." I crossed my heart before exiting.

As I stepped into Sugarbrush Bakery, a refreshing and welcoming atmosphere embraced me. The space oozed a trendy, artsy flair, characterized by its raw brick walls embellished with vibrant artwork and eclectic decorative pieces perching on the shelves. The subtle rhythms of jazz added an air of laid-back sophistication to the scene.

The intoxicating aroma of oven-fresh confections wafted through, a tantalizing blend of melted butter, aromatic vanilla, and caramelized sugar. As I glanced toward the glass counter, a captivating spread of baked delights caught my attention. Artistically shaped sugar cookies, macarons in soft, dreamy colors, and elegant cupcakes topped with detailed fondant patterns were presented like gourmet treasures.

Amelia really did have something special.

"Violet, hey!" She seemed highly excited to see me once she noticed I was there. "I had so much fun last night. Double dating was a blast. Can I get you something?"

"We had a lot of fun too," I said. "It's been a while since Darren has gotten his nose out of the books and let himself have a good time."

I hesitated, not sure what to say. I just decided to go for it.

"I'm actually here to ask you a few questions about one of your employees," I said and glanced around when I didn't see anyone matching the descriptions I'd gotten.

"Sure." She gestured toward the back by jerking her head. "Let's go back to my office."

As Amelia led me through the bakery, I couldn't help but notice how every corner of Sugarbrush Bakery seemed to echo its owner's touch. We finally reached the back office, and when Amelia opened the door, I was instantly drawn into her world.

The office was smaller than I'd expected but made up for its size with an abundance of character.

A large wooden desk, worn from years of use, sat against one wall. The desk's surface was cluttered with scattered paperwork, pastel-colored sticky notes, and design sketches of potential new pastry creations.

The wall behind the desk was adorned with a huge blackboard that bore chalk-drawn diagrams, lists detailing order schedules and special ingredients, and doodles that hinted at upcoming specials for the bakery.

The opposite wall held shelves filled with an array of cookbooks, some of which looked antique, their spines cracked and pages yellowed with age. Interspersed among them stood framed pictures of Amelia with her staff, attending baking workshops or receiving awards. The photos were testaments to her dedication and passion for her craft.

The room was softened by sheer white curtains that allowed a mellow light to filter in, casting the space in a warm, golden hue.

A plush teal armchair sat in one corner. A knitting basket lay beside it, indicating Amelia's penchant for crafting beyond the oven.

The air was scented slightly with vanilla, likely from a reed diffuser that sat atop a filing cabinet, reminding anyone who entered that this office was a space dedicated to the creation of sweet delights.

"You can have a seat." Amelia gestured to the armchair, her voice breaking my trance as I took in the details of her sanctuary. It was a room that felt lived in, brimming with both the business and the heart of Sugarbrush Bakery. "What's up?"

"I understand one of your employees had gone to a chamber meeting and mentioned something about Hippity Hoppity Ranch delivering some of their organic foods, mainly milk, here." As the words left my mouth, I could see her physically push her back against her chair, making her appear taller. "And from the looks of your reaction, you know what I'm talking about."

"Yes." She nodded. "Zephyr Thorne. He told me about the scuffle. In his defense, he had just gotten word that his mama's recipe, which he'd given me, had been taken by another one of our afternoon employees and given to Tara Harden."

"I did hear that, and in light of what has happened to the Hardens—" I paused, not sure how to put my question, so I just blurted it out. "Do you think Zephyr killed them?"

"What? No!" Amelia sounded offended. She popped up and told me to wait right there. Then she left the room and returned with Zephyr himself.

"Tell her where you were all day yesterday," she said.

"I went to Aurelia Falls to meet with an attorney," he said and looked between Amelia and me. "I couldn't use Diffy Delk because he's too involved with the village, and I needed someone who didn't know anyone here in order to sue the Hardens so they'd stop using my mom's recipe for her big show at the Mistletoe Masquerade Ball."

Zephyr ran a hand through his hair, pulling out a small card from his pocket. "If you want to double-check my alibi, here's the attorney's number. He can vouch for our meeting time."

I took the card and scanned the details briefly.

"All right. I'll do that. But if you were there before the Hardens were killed, it would be near impossible for you to return in time to be involved," I said, even though I believed him. I still had to check every lead.

"That's what I've been saying. My issue with the Hardens was about that stolen recipe, not... murder." Zephyr sighed with an expression of mixed frustration and relief.

"And now that Tara is gone, you don't need to sue anymore," I declared.

His eyes reflected a blend of anger and sorrow, and he looked at the floor.

"Yeah. It's a strange kind of justice. All that recipe meant to me was the love and effort my mom poured into it. And now with the ball being relocated to the event center overlooking the mountains, Marianne doesn't need to convince Tara anymore," he said.

"Marianne was pushing Tara to use the recipe? How do you know about the change in venue?" I frowned, puzzled.

Zephyr glanced toward Amelia, who cleared her throat and chimed in, "Marianne approached me about providing desserts for the ball. That's how I knew."

A realization dawned on me. "So, you'd benefit from the change in venue too. With the ball being closer, you'd have an easier time catering."

Amelia shrugged, smiling slightly. "True, but I never wished harm on the Hardens. Business is business, and I keep emotions out of it."

I nodded slowly, making a mental note. With every conversation, the plot seemed to thicken, but at least for now, Zephyr was off my list. The search for the real culprit continued. Since I was already up here, there was no time like the present to stop into this new venue and check it out.

CHAPTER SEVENTEEN

A melia and I stood at the entrance of Sugarbrush Bakery. Just as I turned to leave, she reached out and touched my bandaged hand gently, concern evident in her eyes.

"What happened to your hand, Violet?" she asked.

I hesitated, the memory flashing back.

"Someone threw a brick a me. Strangely enough, it had frosting on it, which is what initially led me to the bakery. I thought Zephyr might have been the culprit, especially with the recipe conflict."

Amelia's brows knitted together as she gave a puzzled frown.

"That's bizarre. Someone's playing a dangerous game here, trying to lead you on a wild goose chase or framing Zephyr, perhaps. But as far as I know, only Tara and Marianne knew about the secret recipe deal," she confirmed.

My heart rate quickened. Marianne. Everything seemed to be pointing her way.

Even Darren had his suspicions about her.

"I need to speak to her," I murmured, my thoughts racing. "And I should check out the new venue."

Amelia nodded. "It's close by, just up the hill. You can't miss it. And she was going up there. Literally, you just missed her when you walked in."

I thanked her, stepped out of the bakery, and looked around. Nestled among the towering trees and slightly elevated on the hill stood the unique silhouette of the venue. It looked like an elaborate treehouse, straight from a fairy tale.

I approached the venue, my shoes crunching on the gravel path leading to it. Made primarily from beautifully polished wood, the structure was an architectural marvel. Massive windows lined the tree house, offering panoramic views. From here, you could overlook the entirety of Holiday Junction, the buildings of the village looking like toy blocks and the glimmering seaside stretching endlessly beyond. The interplay of the dense forest and the vast open sea was breathtaking.

Sturdy wooden beams supported the structure, interwoven seamlessly with the trees around. It was as if nature itself had conspired to build this place. The deck that wrapped around the venue was dotted with elegant chairs and tables so guests could sit, relax, and soak in the view.

Inside, the vaulted ceilings gave the venue an airy, spacious feel, while the soft, ambient lighting created an intimate atmosphere. Though the place was still being set up for the Mistletoe Masquerade Ball, I could already envision the guests dancing the night away, surrounded by nature's beauty.

But even in all this splendor, I couldn't shake off the unease. There were still too many unanswered questions, and Marianne seemed to be at the center of them all. I had to find her and get to the bottom of this.

"Welcome to Elysian Evergreens Venue," a young man said to me. "First time here?"

I turned to see a young man with wavy auburn hair cascading to his shoulders and held in place by a vibrant headband decorated with abstract patterns. He had an array of mismatched earrings, each one a unique piece of art in its own right. His eyes were a deep shade of hazel, framed by long lashes and underlined with a faint touch of kohl. He wore a patchwork jacket, the colors and patterns of each patch telling a different story, over a simple white tee and faded jeans. Around his neck hung an oversized pendant that looked like an artisan's rendition of the moon.

"Sure is," I replied, taking in the young man's bohemian appearance. "You work here?"

He chuckled, revealing a silver tooth. "Yeah, I'm Piers. And you are?"

"Violet." I extended my injured hand instinctively then pulled it back and winced. "Violet Rhinehammer."

He raised an eyebrow but didn't comment.

"So, what do you think of Elysian Evergreens?" he asked, gesturing around.

"It's magnificent. But the name... Elysian Evergreens? What's the story behind it?"

"Ah, the name. 'Elysian' suggests something heavenly or delightful. Evergreens, on the other hand, represent the continuous nature of our celebrations here in Holiday Junction, just like an evergreen tree that remains vibrant throughout the seasons. So, in essence, the venue symbolizes a perpetual haven of delight." Piers grinned, revealing additional unique dental work.

"It certainly feels that way. Thank you, Piers," I said and looked up at the venue again, seeing it in a new light.

With a nod, he gestured toward the entrance, indicating I should explore further. "Enjoy your time, Violet. And if you have any questions, you know where to find me."

"Actually, I'm here to see Marianne Drew," I said.

Upon hearing Marianne's name, Piers perked up, his artsy demeanor shifting to one of understanding and recognition.

"Ah, Marianne! She's got quite a vision for this upcoming event. Does she know you're coming?" he asked.

"Yes," I lied, fishing out a business card from my bag and handing it to him. "I'm with the *Junction Journal*. Marianne contacted me about doing a feature on the Mistletoe Masquerade Ball. I wanted to get some preliminary shots—you know, the 'before' scene—and of course, discuss some details with her."

That much I didn't lie about.

Examining the card briefly, Piers nodded.

"Well, she's here right now, but I can definitely take you to her." He curled his finger for me to follow him.

"Thank you, Piers. I'd appreciate that." I was more than appreciative about getting my eyes on her.

He led me through a massive wooden door intricately carved with various holiday motifs and into a vast space. The interior of Elysian Evergreens was just as breathtaking as its exterior. High ceilings adorned with delicate crystal chandeliers created a sense of grandeur. The gleaming floor, made of polished dark wood, reflected the ambient light from the chandeliers.

But what truly took my breath away was the glass wall on one side of the hall. Stretching from floor to ceiling, it offered an unobstructed, panoramic view of Holiday Junction. The charming village lay sprawling below, and the coastline sparkled in the distance. Even farther out, you could see the hint of the forest and mountainous terrains, painting a serene backdrop.

"Stunning, isn't it? At night, when the village lights up, it's even more magical," Piers remarked when he noticed my awe.

I nodded, snapping a few photos. "This is going to be an exceptional venue for the ball. The view alone is a selling point."

Piers chuckled. "That's the idea. Marianne's always been one for the grand gesture." He clapped his hands. "There she is now."

As I followed Piers's gaze across the hall, my eyes landed on a striking woman who seemed deeply engrossed in conversation with a vendor. She had fiery red hair perfectly styled in waves that cascaded down her back and a posture that commanded attention. Even from this distance, her strong presence was palpable.

When she finally turned to face us, recognition flashed in her eyes. "Violet? Violet Rhinehammer from the *Junction Journal*?"

Caught off guard by her immediate recognition, I nodded at her and extended a hand.

"That would be me. It's a pleasure to finally meet you face-to-face, Marianne," I told her with a smile.

She took my hand in a firm grip, her striking green eyes examining me closely.

"I've seen your photo in the bylines. Didn't expect you here today, though," she confessed, giving my lie away.

I flashed a smile, easing into my professional demeanor.

"Well, I thought I'd come in person to check out the venue and gather some firsthand details. I must say, it's truly impressive. I'm hoping to capture some candid shots while things are still in the planning phase," I said.

Marianne seemed to ponder my reply for a moment before nodding.

"That could work. Authenticity is key, after all." She grinned, looking sinister.

"Would you mind if I got a few shots of the two of you discussing the ball preparations? Just act natural, as if I'm not here," I asked, glancing at Piers.

He looked at Marianne, who shrugged.

"Sure. We can go over the seating chart. That should look sufficiently engrossed and 'authentic,'" she said with a slight smirk.

I couldn't help but chuckle. "Perfect."

As they moved toward a large wooden table laden with layouts and design swatches, I positioned myself to get the best angle, ensuring the impressive glass view was also in frame. While they leaned over the chart, pointing and discussing, I began clicking away, capturing the genuine interactions between Marianne and Piers, with the breathtaking backdrop of Holiday Junction in the distance.

Though our exchange was brief, I sensed that my interactions with Marianne Drew were far from over.

As I took the photos, I thought about the tangled web of relationships in Holiday Junction.

"It's truly a shame," I began, trying to keep my voice casual, "that Tara won't be here to experience this grandeur. She would have loved it."

Marianne looked up from the chart, her expression unreadable. "Yes, it's tragic," she replied evenly.

"I heard there were some disagreements about the venue. People talk, and I heard that she was quite set on not having it here," I continued, unable to resist pushing the envelope a bit further.

"And what exactly are you implying, Violet?" Marianne's posture stiffened, her eyes narrowing slightly.

Not wanting to beat around the bush any longer, I met her gaze head-on. "Did you have anything to do with Tara's death?"

The room grew tense. A pale-faced Piers looked between Marianne and me. She took a deep breath, and for a moment, I wondered if I had overstepped my boundaries.

"Violet, I won't lie. Tara and I had our differences, especially regarding the ball. But to insinuate that I could harm her..." She trailed off, shaking her head. "It's preposterous. She was a colleague, and despite our disagreements, I would never wish her harm."

I held up my hands defensively.

"I had to ask, Marianne. It's my job to uncover the truth. But I also believe in giving everyone a fair chance to share their side," I said.

She took a moment to collect herself then nodded.

"After I found out about Tara's death, I did go see Diffy Delk. I was worried. Given our disagreements about the venue, it wouldn't take much for people to connect dots that shouldn't be connected." Marianne let out a heavy sigh, her shoulders sagging a bit.

Piers looked concerned and placed a reassuring hand on Marianne's shoulder. She gave him a weak smile before continuing.

"Tara was adamant about not moving the venue up here to the art district. She felt it was too... exclusive. But I saw potential here, and I truly believed it would be a game-changer for the town," Marianne said in a passionate voice.

I recalled my earlier observations about the stunning view from Elysian Evergreens and nodded. The place was breathtaking.

"I even took Tara to the Leisure Center to try to appease her," Marianne added with a slight grimace. "I wanted to show her that I was willing to compromise. We could use the Leisure Center for some of the ball's events, making the whole experience more inclusive."

Marianne's mouth opened and shut a few times as if she were trying to find the words to continue.

"Yes, I know that's your mother's establishment, Violet. I should have reached out to you first. I apologize for not doing so." She was at least trying to make amends for my mama thinking she would get Marianne's business.

A swirl of emotions ran through me. On one hand, I was surprised that Marianne was so involved in all the behind-the-scenes of the ball, even considering Millie Kay's. On the other hand, I respected Marianne for trying to compromise.

"I didn't know about that," I replied, softening my voice. "But I do appreciate you trying to bring everything together, despite the obstacles."

Marianne gave a small smile. "It's been a challenging time. But Holiday Junction deserves the best. I just hope we can move forward from all this tragedy and celebrate the season in the spirit of unity."

Her eyes met Piers's. He nodded and walked over to a wooden filing cabinet in the corner. After rummaging briefly, he pulled out a document and handed it to Marianne, who in turn passed it to me.

"I was here, with Piers," she began, pointing at the document I now held. "We were finalizing details and signing the contract for the ball to be held at Elysian Evergreens."

I quickly scanned the document. There they were—the date, the signatures of both Marianne and Piers, and notably, a timestamp indicating the time the contract was notarized. The timing indeed provided Marianne with a solid alibi, placing her far from the scene when the tragic event transpired.

I also noticed the hefty deposit of ten thousand dollars.

Piers cleared his throat. "I can vouch for Marianne. We spent quite a bit of time going over the details and finalizing the contract. It took longer than expected. By the time we wrapped up, it was well past the time of... well, you know," he said.

The sincerity in his eyes was evident, and combined with the contract, it left no doubt in my mind about Marianne's whereabouts.

She had an alibi that would take her right off my list.

Marianne added, her voice soft, "I know the circumstances look suspicious, and with the history between Tara and me, people are bound to talk. But I would never harm anyone, let alone over a disagreement about a venue."

"Thank you for being forthright, Marianne. It's been a day of discovery for me, and I'm just trying to piece everything together." I nodded slowly.

She met my gaze.

"I understand, Violet. Just promise me one thing—you'll find out who did this. Tara didn't deserve this and neither does Holiday Junction," she finished.

I nodded again, now feeling a renewed determination.

"I promise," I said.

Marianne hesitated for a moment, then her professional demeanor returned. "Violet, with everything going on, I almost forgot why you originally came here. Considering the circumstances, it might be more vital than ever to cast the Mistletoe Masquerade Ball in a positive light. We could use some good press right about now. Will you be here to cover it? You can bring a plus-one to the ball. An exclusive invitation with behind-the-scenes footage. After all, it's for charity."

"All right, Marianne. I'll be here. And thank you for the offer." After taking a moment to consider, I agreed. "For the children."

"Thank you, Violet. We need this now more than ever." She offered a smile, albeit a tired one.

I was just stepping out of Elysian Evergreens when my phone buzzed in my pocket. When I pulled it out, I saw Darren's name flash across the screen.

"Hey, Darren," I greeted.

"Violet! Where are you? Haven't heard from you in a bit. Everything all right?" he asked, sounding concerned.

"I'm in the art district," I replied, glancing around. "Could you pick me up? There's a lot to discuss."

"On my way," he responded promptly.

I sighed, looking back at the impressive Elysian Evergreens structure. The day was far from over, and there was still much ground to cover. But with every interaction and piece of information, I felt no closer to untangling the intricate web surrounding the Hardens' mysterious deaths. And now, I was two suspects down. The list was getting shorter.

CHAPTER EIGHTEEN

After Darren had picked me up, we decided to go to Holiday Park. We wanted not only to admire our Merry Maker sign and see how excited people were about the return of the Leaf Dance but also to get one of Nate Lustig's famous Thanksgiving dinner to-go boxes from the Freedom Diner booth.

As soon as we got off the moped, I could already smell the tantalizing aroma of roasted turkey wafting through the air, seasoned to perfection. My mouth watered at the scent alone.

"We could've gone anywhere, but I've been craving this all day," Darren admitted with a chuckle as we approached the booth.

"Sounds like a perfect choice," I said, glancing around to see where we could pop a squat to eat.

"I'll go find us a spot," I said and actually kissed him on the cheek. He was a little surprised by the public affection, but I was fine with it, and his blush and big smile told me he liked it, too, so I did it again before walking away.

Finding a quiet spot, I sat down on the bales of hay.

Darren wasn't too far behind me.

"Wait until you see inside." His eyes twinkled.

He handed me the Styrofoam box. I couldn't believe how heavy it was, but when I opened it, I saw slices of juicy turkey, mashed potatoes drowning in gravy, green beans, and a side of cranberry sauce. From the buttery scent of the potatoes mixed with the herby aroma of the turkey that made my stomach growl, I knew it was a lot of food.

With the bales of hay positioned just right, our knees gently touched. The slight prickling sensation of the hay, its earthy smell grounding us, added to the ambience. We leaned in, making our conversation private amidst the din of the park's festivities.

Taking a bite of the tender turkey, I savored its flavor, allowing myself the momentary distraction before diving into the day's events.

"I spoke to Marianne," I began, glancing up to gauge Darren's reaction.

"And?" he whispered, leaning in closer, his warm breath brushing against my cheek.

"She had an alibi. The contract was signed with Piers right at the time in question. I saw it myself." I sighed and took a sip of my drink, the coolness of the liquid a contrast to the warm, spicy food.

Darren took a thoughtful bite of his food, savoring it for a moment. "So she's off the list too?"

I nodded.

"It seems so. She's just as baffled as we are about Tara's death. Said she even went to apologize to her at the Leisure Center," I said with a mouthful. "And that means you can take back the information to Diffy Delk, and she's cleared."

"Thank you." He smiled and stuck a forkful of stuffing in his mouth. "I've been beating myself up about how to handle this. I'm not so sure I'm going to be a great lawyer."

"You're going to be amazing," I said and saw his eyebrows knot in concentration. "What?"

"If not Marianne, then who...?" His voice trailed off.

We were both lost in thought, trying to piece together the puzzle.

The ambient noise of the park, the distant chatter, children's laughter, and the soft murmur of music surrounded us. But in our small bubble, as we were seated on the hay bales with our plates of food and the list of unanswered questions, everything else felt distant.

"All isn't lost yet." I pulled out my notebook, and as we ate, I glanced at the list of suspects, which was really down to one likely name. "Daphne Marsh is still on my list."

"From the thrift store?" he asked.

"Yes. Fern said she could get me in front of Daphne, which reminds me." I set the piece of buttery biscuit in the box, pulled my cell phone from my bag, and sent Fern a quick text to ask if we could go by there tomorrow. "I would love for all of this to be figured out by Friendsgiving."

Darren snorted.

"What?" I asked, picking the biscuit back up.

"That's not tomorrow but the next day." He looked as if he didn't think I could do it. "Whoa." He put his hand out, his biscuit in it. "I see that look on your face, and I do not underestimate Violet Rhinehammer in any way. Here, have my biscuit as a peace offering."

I took it too.

His jaw dropped as if he didn't think I would.

"We'll figure it out," Darren said, placing his hand over mine, offering comfort. I looked into his eyes, seeing the determination and unwavering support.

"Yes we will," I whispered back, squeezing his hand.

"Are we going to go to your house tonight?" Darren asked.

"We can if you want to," I said, shrugging. "As long as we get to hang out."

"I have that contract Diffy asked me to draw up between Millie Kay and Fern for the Leisure Center," he said and then looked down at my hand. "But if you aren't feeling up to it."

"No, no." I waved my hand around. "I'm fine. But I still am determined to find out who on earth did this."

"And you really think Zephyr Thorne didn't do it?" He was questioning what Amelia and Zephyr had told me as well as the evidence that proved he was in Aurelia Falls.

"I can't believe he wouldn't use Diffy. I think I'll have to go out on my own after law school and start my own firm." There wasn't an ounce of kidding in his voice.

"And where on earth would you make your office?" I asked, knowing space was limited around here. "The art district? The back of the jiggle joint?" I joked.

His face stilled.

"I could." His brows rose as if I had just turned on a lightbulb in his head. "Didn't you tell me your friend's husband, Mae from home, has his office in the back of a coffee shop?"

"Yeah." I nodded. "You've got the mind of an elephant."

"What?" His head jerked, his nose curled, and he smiled.

"You know. Elephants have large memory capacities." It rolled off my tongue. "Trust me, I have no idea how I retain really odd facts."

We finished up our meal and stood, with Darren stretching out his tall frame. The park around us was now a hive of activity. The setting sun's last hues painted a picturesque backdrop as string lights began to twinkle overhead. The fiddles and banjos struck up a lively tune, and a section of the park transformed into an impromptu dance floor. Couples young and old took to it with enthusiasm, their feet stomping in rhythm, skirts swirling, and laughter filling the air.

As we meandered our way back toward where the moped was parked, snippets of excited conversation reached our ears.

"I've got my dress all ready for the Leaf Dance tomorrow," a young girl declared to her friend, the gleam of excitement in her eyes unmistakable. An older couple walked hand in hand, the woman reminiscing. "Every year, the Leaf Dance always takes me back to our younger days."

Darren leaned down and whispered, "Looks like the Leaf Dance is the highlight for many. Maybe we should join in the fun?"

I chuckled. "After today, a dance might be just what we need to lift our spirits."

He smiled, his arm wrapping around my waist. "Then let's not miss it. After all, we are the Merry Makers."

Once we approached the moped, we donned our helmets and

revved up the engine. As we pulled away from the park, the sounds of square dancing and joyous chatter became a distant melody, but the spirit of the festival and the anticipation for the upcoming Leaf Dance lingered in our hearts.

Still, someone was lurking out there.

Watching me.

Waiting.

I felt like they were about to try to make another move to keep me quiet.

CHAPTER NINETEEN

Just like the day before, I got up early and headed to the office. Only this time I took my mace and remembered to be very vigilant to the world around me. My decision to go right at dawn didn't hurt either.

The hand injury I'd sustained from falling on Mama's coffee mug hurt more than the knot on my head, but that was nothing a good cup of coffee from Brewing Beans couldn't help.

With every step toward Brewing Beans, I felt the comforting aroma of coffee drawing me in. The warm light from inside the café poured onto the sidewalk, giving me a sense of coziness on this crisp morning. I pushed the door open, and the familiar chime announced my arrival.

Inside, Brewing Beans felt like Thanksgiving was in full swing. The walls were adorned with golden leaves and orange twinkle lights, while pumpkins of all sizes sat in clusters around the room. Tucked into one corner was a Christmas tree, but instead of traditional ornaments, it was decorated with fall leaves, miniature pumpkins, and quirky coffee mugs.

Hazelynn, the owner, stood behind the counter, engaged in a lively conversation with a customer. Her eyes darted toward me, and a mischievous twinkle appeared in them. Clearly, she had some juicy tidbits to share.

As I waited, she handed the customer their drink, her words flowing faster than the coffee from her pot. The customer, sensing her eagerness to move on, quickly took their beverage and left.

Hazelynn practically jumped toward me, her excitement barely contained.

"Violet! Honey, have you found out any more about the Hardens? Such a tragedy! But between you and me"—she leaned in, her voice dropping to a whisper—"I always felt something like this might happen. There's been so much drama around that family."

I humored her, knowing full well her penchant for the dramatic. "Really, Hazelynn? What makes you say that?"

She leaned even more closely, her voice barely above a whisper. "Did you know the Hardens went every year during the parole hearings of that boy—what's his name, the one who killed their son—to ensure he stayed locked up? I wonder how he feels about it all. Not that he deserves to feel anything."

Before I could inquire further, a gruff voice interrupted us.

"Hazelynn! Stop your yammerin' and pour the coffee!" Hershal Hudson, Hazelynn's husband, yelled.

Hazelynn rolled her eyes but turned to attend to her other customers.

"That's Hershal for you. Always thinking of the next dollar. Anyway, honey, I've got to run. But you take care. After what I heard, you've hit a button." She looked at my hand.

I smiled, grabbing my freshly poured coffee. "Thanks, Hazelynn. I will."

As I sipped the hot brew, I pondered her words. The tangled web surrounding the Hardens was growing more intricate by the day, and every tidbit of information, even from the town gossip, could prove invaluable.

Again, this was the second time someone had reminded me about the man sitting in prison for killing the Hardens' son. He might not have done them in himself, but I sure did bet he had a person on the outside who could do his dirty deeds.

Sipping on the comforting warmth of my coffee, I made my way toward Holiday Park. Although the day's festival activities hadn't kicked off, you could feel the anticipation in the air. Fall was in its prime, with trees showcasing an array of golden and amber hues. The weather promised a perfect fall day, and the sun, though not entirely up yet, cast a warm, inviting glow.

The path soon led me to the seaside. From there, I could see the proud silhouette of the lighthouse, standing tall against the canvas of the morning sky. The moped was gone, which only confirmed my thoughts that Darren was already at Diffy's office, getting an early start.

The sound of waves crashing against the shore, coupled with the scent of the salty sea, was almost therapeutic. But that serenity was contrasted by the sharp chill of the ocean breeze. I pulled my jacket more tightly around me, the gusts whipping my hair and amplifying the cold.

Walking this path was always a journey of mixed emotions. The tranquility of the sea, the beauty of the changing leaves, and the excitement of the festival juxtaposed against the mysteries and dangers entangled with me. But each step forward was a step toward the truth.

Drawing closer to the office, I felt my mind refocus on the issues at hand. The death of the Hardens, the gossip, and the ever-growing list of suspects. And now, the reminder of a man behind bars with a vendetta.

Today was going to be another long day, but I was ready.

Once I entered the office, the first thing that caught my eye was the murder board. Papers, photos, and colored strings formed a chaotic yet organized tapestry of information and connections. Without wasting any time, I headed straight for it, determined to update our findings.

Under the section marked "Sugarbrush Bakery," I pinned a new card labeled "Zephyr's Alibi" and scribbled down the key details, making sure to note the time and day he was at the bakery, and the rock-solid alibi Daisy had provided.

Next, I turned my attention to Marianne's section. I took a fresh card, labeled it "Marianne's Alibi," and started listing the salient points. "Contract signed at Elysian Evergreens," I wrote, followed by "Witness: Piers," to ensure we knew who vouched for her.

Just as I was about to add another note, the office door creaked open. Without even turning, I called out, "Radley, grab a cup of coffee. We've got a long day ahead."

But it wasn't Radley's familiar voice that answered. Instead, a more authoritative, deeper voice responded, "Not unless Chief Strickland's now been demoted to fetching coffee."

I whipped around and found Chief Strickland standing at the doorway, an amused smirk playing on his lips. My heart did a quick tap dance against my ribs; this was unexpected.

"Chief," I replied, slightly caught off guard, "what brings you here so early?"

Chief Strickland took a moment to observe the murder board, scanning each section meticulously. He gave an approving nod, seemingly impressed with the progress I'd made so far.

"How are you feeling after yesterday?" he inquired genuinely.

Without thinking about it, I touched the back of my head.

"I've had better days. A bruise or two, but I'll survive. More determined now than ever," I said.

His gaze was steady.

"The brick didn't give us any fingerprints, but the white residue you mentioned was indeed frosting. Seems you were right about the bakery," he remarked.

That revelation sent a shiver down my spine. A simple brick and a smear of frosting had added another layer of mystery to the case.

"Both Zephyr and Marianne dropped by the station yesterday. They wanted to make sure we knew they didn't have any part in the Hardens' deaths. They mentioned their meeting with you," he continued.

"I didn't intend for them to feel the need to go to the station." I sighed, feeling a bit embarrassed.

"Sometimes, people just want to clear their names, especially in a small town where rumors spread like wildfire." He shrugged.

I nodded then took a deep breath.

"Chief, have you considered the possibility of the man in prison, the one who killed the Hardens' son? Could he have orchestrated a hit from the inside?" I asked.

Chief Strickland's casual expression became more intense.

"We did consider it. It's a valid lead, but proving that and finding connections from the inside out... That's going to be challenging," he admitted.

"I'm up for a challenge," I stated firmly.

"You are not up for it because I've already got guys on it." He smirked. "I wanted to stop by and see how you were today, tell you about the brick, and thank you for stepping in yesterday morning with Tara. The pictures were great."

I met his gaze. "I want the truth, and I want justice for the Hardens. I hope you give me the scoop for the *Junction Journal* when you get whoever did this arrested."

"I will if you promise me you're going to stop snooping around now. Let yourself heal and enjoy yourself today at the festival and tomorrow at your Friendsgiving." His words didn't sound like him.

"Ah." I lifted my chin in the air. "Did your wife send you? Or your son?"

"The first one. Louise told me I couldn't put you in danger. She needed you here." He tapped the doorframe and turned to leave. "You didn't hear me tell you that either."

I laughed. Through the office window, I watched him get into his cruiser . Then I turned to the murder board. It was practically useless to me, but instead of taking the time to clean it off, I went over to my desk, where I brought up the computer. I needed to upload my photos from yesterday's Thanksgiving Festival events and add something to the online newspaper for our readers today.

As I began transferring the photos, each image seemed to tell a unique story of yesterday's festivities. The first series showcased the golden hour of early morning, when runners from the 5k Turkey Trot appeared, their expressions varying from sheer determination to cheerful camaraderie.

Then came the images from the log-rolling competition held at the nearby lake. The contestants had to balance on floating logs, trying to knock their opponents off into the water without falling in as well. The series captured the intense concentration, skill, and occasional splash. There were shots of crowd reactions too—spectators cheering on their favorites and wincing empathetically when someone took an unexpected dip.

Another set of pictures showed the pie-eating contest. The participants' sheer joy and playful competitiveness made me chuckle. Faces smeared with blueberries, cherries, and whipped cream, eyes wide in surprise or narrowed in determination, all captured in high definition.

I loved Radley's angle on a lot of them. And I was beginning to really like him. He made a good addition to the team, and I was beyond thrilled Amelia turned out to be exactly the person I thought she was.

Amazing!

I turned back to the candid shots of families enjoying their picnics, children playing traditional games, and couples walking hand in hand, taking in the sights and sounds of the festival. Each image held the essence of the holiday spirit—the celebration of love, gratitude, and the sense of community.

There were so many it was hard to decide which ones to put in the online article. Then I got the great idea to throw all the photos into a festival gallery. That was easy with a click of a button.

Among more of the photos, a particularly heartwarming scene caught my eye. This one showed elderly couples dancing at the square dance. Their steps might have been slower, but the joy in their movements and the sparkle in their eyes spoke of young love.

Lastly, the shots from the arts and crafts stalls showcased the town's artistic talent. Handmade trinkets, intricate embroideries, and beautiful paintings all held stories of their own.

Each photo brought back a memory, a sound, a smell from yesterday. I moved the mouse over to the photos I'd taken the day before and saw the lovable images of the Hippity Hoppity Ranch, the

Ceramic Celebration, and the amazing Thanksgiving display Nadia had made.

I zipped those into the festival gallery, which I was shocked to see contained over one hundred photos already. We hadn't even gone to today's festival activities.

My mind circled to the Leaf Dance. Though it would be my first, everyone who had grown up here was very excited to see it was back.

With all the photos picked for the article, I put my hands on the keys, and before too long, I hit Send, publishing it.

A Day of Celebrations: Highlights from Holiday Junction's Thanksgiving Festival!

From the athletic prowess displayed at the 5k Turkey Trot and log-rolling competition to the sheer delight of pie-eating contests, yesterday's Thanksgiving Festival showcased the heart and spirit of our community. Take a visual journey with us as we share some of our favorite moments. Whether you've attended in person or are viewing from afar, these snapshots are sure to evoke the spirit of gratitude and festivity! Be sure to check the online festival gallery. You just might see your smiling face in it.

As I was finishing up with the uploads, the door creaked open, and Radley's familiar silhouette filled the entrance.

"Hey, Violet. Saw Chief Strickland leaving. Everything okay?" he asked, his eyes showing genuine concern.

"Hey, Radley," I said without looking up from the screen. "Yeah, everything's fine. Just updating him on the case, as usual."

Radley approached, taking a closer look at my bandaged hand.

"How's the hand? And your head this morning?" he inquired, a wry grin forming on his lips.

I rolled my eyes, stretching out my fingers.

"The hand's not too bad, though gripping things is a bit of a challenge. As for my head, well, it's seen better days, but I'll live." I smiled.

He chuckled. "Always the optimist. But seriously, you should take it easy. There's a lot going on, and with the festival today... maybe take a breather?"

"I've had enough breathers, Radley." My brows rose because he wasn't good at keeping information from Chief Strickland, who had probably instructed Radley to keep me safe and not snoop.

"Anyways, there's the list of events." I pointed at the other white-board. "And there's a new suspect."

I pointed at the other white board, on which I'd written "Hardens' son's killer."

"I want you to snoop around and see what you can find out about their son." I reached for my phone when I got a text. It was Fern. "I'm going to go meet Fern at Festive Finds and look into Daphne Marsh."

"And you think the guy in prison is the Hardens' killer?" Radley asked.

"I think he could have ties from the outside who could get revenge, especially since I heard this morning from Hazelynn Hudson that the Hardens show up to this guy's parole hearings every year in order to make sure he stays in jail." I grabbed my bag and threw my phone inside. "I want everything. Where he's from. Parents. Siblings. Children. Spouse. Everything."

"All right." He started to walk out of my office. "Oh, would you mind stopping by Sugarbrush at some point today and grabbing some of the cookies for tomorrow's Friendsgiving?" he asked and put his hands together as if he were begging me. "I was going to go, but you've got me doing this."

"I can probably get Fern up there." I didn't commit but didn't say no either. I would make it happen somehow.

With my bag tossed over my shoulder, I headed out the door, confident Radley would find out all the details.

The trolley came into view, and from a distance, I could already spot Goldie's outfit for the day.

Today, she donned a vibrant orange skirt decorated with hand-painted fall leaves, a matching blouse with ruffles at the collar and cuffs, and a wreath made of golden twigs and autumn flowers crowning her hair. She looked every inch the embodiment of fall.

As I climbed aboard, it was evident that the trolley was more packed than usual. It buzzed with the chatter of excited tourists, their eyes wide as they took in Holiday Junction's festive atmosphere.

Goldie maneuvered masterfully through the crowd, handing out brochures and answering questions with her usual sunny demeanor.

"Ladies and gentlemen," she announced with a theatrical flourish, "for those of you who are new to our town, welcome to Holiday Junction! Home of the famous Merry Maker and where we love to celebrate every single holiday."

Whispers of intrigue filled the air, and a few tourists leaned forward, clearly captivated.

"The Merry Maker," Goldie continued, "holds one of the most vital roles in our town. Each festival, they secretly determine the location of our grand finale. There's a large sign for every holiday. And wherever that sign is posted, that's where our celebration concludes. It's one of our most cherished traditions. Keeps everyone guessing! This year, I'll point out the big leaf structure that will end the festival tonight at the Leaf Dance."

I could hear murmurs of excitement and anticipation from the tourists. They seemed fascinated, perhaps even more determined to find out where this festival's climax would take place.

A few minutes passed, filled with more of Goldie's cheerful stories about Holiday Junction and the history of the dance, and then the trolley came to a smooth stop.

"Festive Finds," she announced, winking at me as I stood up.

"Thanks, Goldie," I said, stepping off the trolley and taking a deep breath, preparing myself for the next task in my investigation.

The chime of the doorbell rang out as I entered Festive Finds, and I was immediately enveloped by the cozy ambience of the store. Rich aromas of cinnamon and vanilla wafted from the back, and the light acoustic music playing in the background added to the homey vibe. The walls were adorned with colorful streamers and twinkling fairy lights, highlighting the various festive items on display.

My eyes quickly located Fern near the changing rooms. Her arms were overloaded with various dresses, blouses, and skirts. She was animatedly discussing something with a sales assistant, probably about the right size or style.

"Violet!" Fern exclaimed when she saw me, her voice filled with excitement. She gracefully navigated through the maze of clothes racks, her haul still hanging from her arm. "You're just in time! Look at these beauties I've found. They'll be perfect for pageant training. The girls can learn to walk, sit, and even stand with grace in these outfits."

I chuckled at her enthusiasm.

"You always have an eye for this stuff, Fern. But didn't you text me about some information?" I asked. I was there strictly to learn about Daphne and Tara's relationship now that I knew Daphne had a vested interest in the property next to the Leisure Center where Tara's son's body had been found.

"Yes, I did," Fern replied, her eyes sparkling with mischief. "And that information is tied to this lovely lady right here." She motioned toward a tall, slender woman with raven-black hair and elegant features. "Violet, meet Daphne Marsh."

Daphne extended a graceful hand, her nails impeccably manicured. "Pleased to meet you, Violet," she said, her voice as smooth as silk. "I've heard a lot about you."

"All good things, I hope," I replied with a smile, shaking her hand. She exuded a confidence that was hard to miss.

"Oh, most definitely," Daphne responded with a wink. "And I understand you have some questions for me?"

I glanced at Fern, who gave me a subtle nod, confirming that Daphne was in the know. Taking a deep breath, I mentally prepared myself for the conversation ahead.

"Violet, Daphne Marsh," Fern said with a hint of formality, "owner of Festive Finds."

"I've followed your stories in the *Junction Journal*. Are you doing an exposé on this whole situation?" Daphne gave me a nice compliment.

"Not exactly. This has gotten a bit... personal." I couldn't help but show my bruised hand slightly.

Daphne's intense eyes darted to my hand, concern evident in them. "I see. That looks painful."

"Tell me about your relationship with Tara." Nodding, I tried to steer the conversation back.

"We were once neighbors. However, my interest in the land next to the Leisure Center strained our relationship. She opposed its development, especially after her son's incident." Daphne heaved a weary sigh.

"So there was conflict?" I asked.

Daphne met my gaze.

"Yes, but it wasn't hostile. A few others and I planned to attend the luncheon to support Tara. We wanted to help her find some form of peace," she said with a frown, the tone of her voice dipping as she spoke.

She paused, looking pensive.

"The last I spoke with Tara was when I informed her I'd miss the luncheon. An employee had fallen sick, leaving Festive Finds unattended."

I considered her words. "So you were here during the murders?"

Daphne nodded. "I was. But what disturbs me is how Tara sounded during our call. She and Albert were arguing."

I raised an eyebrow, intrigued.

"You think Tara might've harmed Albert?" I asked, thinking Daphne had revealed a possible angle I never even considered.

"Could she have, in a fit of rage, killed him and then... taken her own life from the guilt?" Daphne voiced her concern.

The possibility settled on me, adding another layer of complexity to the ever-twisting story of the Hardens.

"Thank you for your time." Clearly, I had some more digging around to do, and I couldn't go back to the office to tell Radley without bringing him his Friendsgiving cookies. "Fern, are you ready?"

"Yeah." She nodded. "I'll pay for these and meet you outside," she said, following Daphne up to the register as I walked outside again.

I stepped out into the cool, crisp air, and as I waited for Fern, I considered our next move. "Hey, Fern," I began as she caught up with me, "how about we head up to the art district? Maybe you'll find some things for your pageant school there."

Her eyes sparkled with excitement. "Oh, I'd love to! I've been meaning to check out some new suppliers and boutiques. Plus, I heard there's a place that's selling unique costume jewelry. Perfect for my classes!"

I chuckled. "All right, then, it's settled."

We approached the trolley stop just as one was pulling up. The golden bells jingled, announcing its arrival, and we boarded. Too bad this wasn't Goldie's route. I had really enjoyed hearing her tell her tales about Holiday Junction to tourists this morning. She'd done that with me when I first moved to the town.

As the trolley chugged along, Fern and I chatted about the various shops in the art district and what she was hoping to find.

"We'll stop at Sugarbrush Bakery first," I reminded her. "I promised Radley I'd grab some cookies for Friendsgiving."

"Oh, I've been craving their pumpkin-spiced macarons," Fern replied with a smile. "This is going to be a treat."

The trolley came to a gentle stop outside the Sugarbrush Bakery, and the aroma of freshly baked pastries greeted us. The bakery was adorned with autumnal decorations—pumpkins on the windowsills, strands of golden leaves hanging from the ceiling, and an assortment of pies that made my mouth water.

"Shall we?" I said, holding the door open for Fern.

She nodded eagerly. "Let's!"

I was about to push the bakery door open when a chime came from my bag. Pulling my phone out, I saw Radley's name flashing on the screen.

"Hold on a moment, Fern," I said, answering the call. "Hey, Radley. What's up?"

I could hear the shuffle of papers in the background. "Got some info on that guy you wanted details on. The one who killed the Hardens' son."

I leaned against the wall outside the bakery, listening intently.

"He was very young when he got into jail, so he's been there for a while now. Grown quite a bit older in that place," Radley began. "Interesting bit, he's an only child. Raised by a single mother. She's an art teacher."

My eyebrows rose. "An art teacher? Anything else?"

"That's where it gets a bit weird. I couldn't find much about her online. It's like she's made an effort to remain hidden or something." Radley sighed. "Only articles about him."

That definitely piqued my curiosity. "Any idea where she might be teaching?"

Radley hesitated for a moment. "No specifics yet. But I've got a lead or two I'm following up on. Figured you'd want to know."

"Thanks, Radley," I replied, my mind racing. "What was the man's name?" I asked, since we'd yet to find out.

"Leo Fitch," he said.

"You said Finch?" I jerked back at the sound of a golf cart whizzing by.

"Fit-ch," Radley sounded out.

"Leo Fitch," I repeated. "His mom's name?"

"Umm… Nina Fitch," he said, making my heart stop.

"Radley." I glanced over at the Winston Art Gallery. "I need you to do me a favor because I'm at the Sugarbrush Bakery, getting your cookies."

"Of course." He laughed. "What's your favor?"

"I did an article on a local artist, Nadia Finch, and I want you to look into her background," I said. I started to walk over to the gallery, Fern close on my heels as we frogged our way across the street, in and out of traffic. "Let me know what you find."

CHAPTER TWENTY

The Winston Art Gallery's vibrant colors and diverse artwork surrounded me as I walked in, the soft murmurs of conversation from a few visitors filling the space. Fern immediately gravitated toward a bright contemporary piece, her eyes wide with admiration.

I, however, had a different goal in mind. My heart raced in my chest as I began to search for Nadia. The suspicion, the connections—they all led me to her. And if my instincts were right, confronting her would not be easy.

As I ventured deeper into the gallery, I caught a glimpse of Nadia, her signature raven-black hair pulled back, revealing an elegant profile. She was examining one of her own pieces, seemingly lost in thought.

"Nadia?" Approaching her, I tried to keep my voice steady.

She turned, her expression neutral at first. But when she saw me, her features softened.

"Ah, Violet. Back for more insights into my art?" she asked.

Before I could reply, she seemed to register the tension on my face and the edge in my voice. She glanced briefly at my injured hand. Her expression turned from one of casual greeting to one of understanding.

"You've figured it out, haven't you?" she whispered, an air of resignation in her voice.

I hesitated for a moment, trying to find the right words.

"I think I have," I admitted.

Nadia looked at my hand again.

"I didn't want to kill you. I just wanted to send a message. But clearly, that wasn't enough." Her voice, previously soft and friendly, became chillingly cold.

Before I could react, she produced a gun and pointed it directly at me.

My heart sank as the situation pressed down on me. I thought of all the moments that had led me here, all the clues, all the pieces that connected. And in the blink of an eye, it felt as though it could all end.

Surrounded by the vivid artwork that I had once admired, I was now confronted by its creator, a woman hiding a world of grief and anger behind her brushstrokes. The gun in Nadia's hand trembled, a testament to the storm of emotions inside her.

"Your article," Nadia began, her voice shaky. "It showed the world a side of me, a mother who creates, a mother who loves. But did you ever think that same love could drive someone to do unimaginable things?"

I swallowed hard, my mind racing for an escape, for a way to get out of the gallery alive. "Nadia," I said, trying to keep my voice steady, "why are you doing this?"

She burst into a bitter laugh. "The whole village turned its back on my son. They judged him, vilified him. Yes, he made a terrible mistake, but he was young. It was an accident. They made him out to be a monster, and that ruined him!"

Images of Nadia's artwork flashed in my mind. Had there been hints? Messages? "Your art," I whispered. "Was it a reflection of your feelings toward the Hardens?"

Her eyes glistened with unshed tears. "Every brushstroke, every sculpture was filled with my grief and my rage. How dare they try to keep my son locked away? I wanted to show them pain. So I confronted them, begged them to stop attending the parole hearings. But they wouldn't listen. They said they'd never let Leo out. That's when I... I lost control."

The heaviness of her confession was like a punch to the gut. The revelation created a whirlwind of emotions within me. I felt empathy for the grieving mother, but the horror of her actions was inescapable.

Seeing my shocked expression, she continued, "I thought that by getting rid of them, my son would have a chance. But nothing changed. The village's view of him remained unchanged, and now my hands were stained too."

My heart hammered against my ribs, echoing the frenzied pace of my thoughts. I could almost taste the metallic tang of fear on my tongue. I instinctively took a small step back and placed a decorative pedestal between Nadia and me, but she only tightened her grip on the gun.

"I wanted to start fresh, be close to Leo, be there for him." Nadia's voice grew louder, more desperate. "I thought by changing my name, by immersing myself in my art, I could find some solace, some forgiveness. But the village's whispers, their glances—they never stopped. Everywhere I turned, I was reminded of that fateful night."

I nodded slowly, trying to keep her engaged, stalling for time.

"But why come after me, Nadia? Why the brick? I wrote about your talent, your art." I had put two and two together about the frosting on the brick, the frosting she used in the Thanksgiving piece, and now her name change.

"Your article brought too much attention. Suddenly, everyone was talking about Nadia Finch. I didn't want anyone digging, discovering my connection to Leo, finding out what I did. I wanted to send you a message to back off, but you didn't get it." She smirked bitterly. "And I certainly didn't want you to dig around in the Hardens' murders."

My breathing grew shallow. I felt sweat forming on my brow, and my fingers twitched with the urge to do something, anything, to escape the confines of the gallery. "I had no idea, Nadia," I said, trying to reason with her. "I just wanted to showcase your talent."

"Talent? All of that is just a facade. Every piece I created was a scream, a cry for my son, a rage against the world that took him from me." She released a cold, humorless laugh.

I could see the pain etched deeply into the lines of her face. The burden of her secrets seemed to press down on her, warping her once vibrant spirit into something darker.

Nadia's eyes glistened with tears, but her grip on the gun remained unwavering. "You want to know how? How I avenged my son?" Her voice was a mix of anger and sorrow.

I nodded, each beat of my heart punctuating the silent prayers coursing through my mind.

"Albert and Tara were responsible for the ruining of Leo's life," Nadia began. "They may not have been the ones to throw the switch, but their constant presence at his parole hearings, their unyielding quest for vengeance, ensured my boy never had a chance. So I decided they needed to understand what it felt like to lose everything. He was sorry for what he'd done, and they didn't care."

She paused, drawing a shaky breath. "I confronted Albert at the Leisure Center. I wanted him to see me, know me, recognize the mother of the boy whose life he ruined. We fought, and in the heat of the moment, I pushed him. He stumbled down those steps, and his last moments were filled with fear and regret."

The confession chilled me to the bone, but I needed to hear everything.

"And Tara?" I prompted, despite the dread pooling in my stomach.

Nadia's face contorted in anguish.

"Tara was at home. I didn't intend to... but when she saw me, the shock on her face, the realization of what I told her I had done to Albert —it pushed me over the edge. I smothered her, wanted her to feel the bulk of my grief, my anger, my love for my son pressing down on her."

Tears streamed down her face, but the hand she held the gun in was firm.

"They needed to know the pain they caused. But it didn't bring Leo back. It didn't ease my suffering," she confessed.

I tried to summon any words that could defuse the situation, to break through to the tormented woman before me.

As she continued speaking, I discreetly fumbled for my phone in my pocket, hoping to send a quick message to Radley. But before I could even unlock the device, she noticed.

"Trying to call for help?" Nadia sneered. "No one's going to save you."

My heart plummeted, but I refused to give in to despair. I kept my gaze steady, trying to find the woman behind the rage, the artist behind the pain.

I took in a sharp breath, my eyes darting between Nadia's sneering face and the exit. Every instinct screamed for me to run, but my legs felt glued to the floor. The cold, metallic taste of fear filled my mouth.

Out of the corner of my eye, I saw a subtle movement.

Fern.

My heart raced even faster but not from fear. It was hope. The dim light from the gallery's side window caught the glint of something sharp. A stiletto heel.

Fern had come to my rescue, proving that sometimes, our saviors came from the most unexpected places. The rest, as they say, was history.

She was removing the stiletto with great finesse, with the kind of grace and poise only years in pageantry could teach. The shoe dangled precariously from her fingers, just for a split second, before it became a weapon in her hand.

Nadia didn't see it coming.

Time seemed to slow, every detail magnified. I could hear the soft rustling of Fern's dress, see the determined set of her jaw, the glint of determination in her eyes. It was like watching a dancer, each move deliberate, practiced, and yet infused with a raw, desperate energy.

In a blur of motion that belied her graceful movements just moments before, Fern lunged at Nadia. The shoe's pointed heel connected solidly with the side of Nadia's head. A sickening thud followed, and Nadia crumpled to the floor, the threat of her gun gone limp in her hand.

The room was suddenly very quiet, save for the ragged breaths Fern and I were taking.

"There are so many things you learn in pageant school." Fern panted, a hint of a smirk playing on her lips as she dangled the high heel from her finger. "Including self-defense."

All I could do was shake my head.

CHAPTER TWENTY-ONE

Exclusive for the Junction Journal
When Leaves Danced and Justice Prevailed

By The Merry Maker

T he *Autumn Leaf Dance was nothing short of spectacular this year. Set against a backdrop of golden hues and crisp fall air, Holiday Junction's latest location choice turned out to be a massive hit, leaving an indelible mark on the memories of all who attended. Kudos to those responsible for the venue selection! A round of applause is in order, don't you think?*

In the spirit of gratitude and togetherness, Junction witnessed its first-ever Friendsgiving at the Leisure Center. The turnout? Heartwarming! The food? Delectable! The atmosphere? Brimming with gratitude. A special nod to Millie Kay Rhinehammer for her role in orchestrating such a beautiful gathering. Here's hoping Friendsgiving becomes an annual affair, reminding us of the ties that bind us.

But beyond the festivities, a darker tale unraveled, and justice was served, not by our local police force alone but by the relentless drive of our very own

Violet Rhinehammer. It's not every day a journalist unmasks a killer while simultaneously uniting two clashing districts! Not only did Violet's efforts ensure that justice prevailed, but she's also single-handedly championed a cause that might just see our beloved village, torn between tradition and innovation, knit back together as one cohesive unit.

Speaking of uniting, the town is all abuzz about the upcoming Mistletoe Masquerade Ball! Can you believe it? The ball will be hosted in no other place than our burgeoning art district. Now, if that isn't a symbol of our two worlds coming together, I don't know what is.

In other joyous news, during the grand reveal of the Mistletoe Masquerade Ball, our dear Marianne Drew was honored with the Key to the Village. A well-deserved accolade for a woman who's devoted so much of her time and energy to making Holiday Junction what it is today and raising all the money for our children. Even though the ball isn't here yet, we hear the money raised so far has surpassed all the previous years.

Before I sign off, dear Junction Journal *readers, I'd like to drop a tiny hint for the season's festivities. Stay tuned for where the grand Yuletide celebrations will culminate. Let's just say it's going to be a holiday like no other. Keep your eyes peeled and your ears to the ground. The Merry Maker promises you won't want to miss the final hurrah of this Christmas season.*

As always, keep the spirit alive and remember to find joy in the little things.

Stay Merry,

The Merry Maker

THE END

If you enjoyed reading this book as much as I enjoyed writing it then be sure to return to the Amazon page and leave a review.

Go to Tonyakappes.com for a full reading order of my novels and while there join my newsletter. You can also find links to Facebook, Instagram and Goodreads.

BOOKS BY TONYA
SOUTHERN HOSPITALITY WITH A SMIDGEN OF HOMICIDE

Camper & Criminals Cozy Mystery Series

All is good in the camper-hood until a dead body shows up in the woods.

BEACHES, BUNGALOWS, AND BURGLARIES
DESERTS, DRIVING, & DERELICTS
FORESTS, FISHING, & FORGERY
CHRISTMAS, CRIMINALS, AND CAMPERS
MOTORHOMES, MAPS, & MURDER
CANYONS, CARAVANS, & CADAVERS
HITCHES, HIDEOUTS, & HOMICIDES
ASSAILANTS, ASPHALT & ALIBIS
VALLEYS, VEHICLES & VICTIMS
SUNSETS, SABBATICAL AND SCANDAL
TENTS, TRAILS AND TURMOIL
KICKBACKS, KAYAKS, AND KIDNAPPING
GEAR, GRILLS & GUNS
EGGNOG, EXTORTION, AND EVERGREEN
ROPES, RIDDLES, & ROBBERIES
PADDLERS, PROMISES & POISON
INSECTS, IVY, & INVESTIGATIONS
OUTDOORS, OARS, & OATH
WILDLIFE, WARRANTS, & WEAPONS
BLOSSOMS, BBQ, & BLACKMAIL
LANTERNS, LAKES, & LARCENY
JACKETS, JACK-O-LANTERN, & JUSTICE
SANTA, SUNRISES, & SUSPICIONS
VISTAS, VICES, & VALENTINES
ADVENTURE, ABDUCTION, & ARREST
RANGERS, RVS, & REVENGE

CELEBRATE GOOD CRIMES!

FOUR LEAF FELONY
MOTHER'S DAY MURDER
A HALLOWEEN HOMICIDE
NEW YEAR NUISANCE
CHOCOLATE BUNNY BETRAYAL
FOURTH OF JULY FORGERY
SANTA CLAUSE SURPRISE
APRIL FOOL'S ALIBI

Kenni Lowry Mystery Series

**_Mysteries so delicious it'll make your mouth water and leave you
hankerin' for more._**

FIXIN' TO DIE
SOUTHERN FRIED
AX TO GRIND
SIX FEET UNDER
DEAD AS A DOORNAIL
TANGLED UP IN TINSEL
DIGGIN' UP DIRT
BLOWIN' UP A MURDER
HEAVENS TO BRIBERY

Magical Cures Mystery Series

Welcome to Whispering Falls where magic and mystery collide.

A CHARMING CRIME
A CHARMING CURE
A CHARMING POTION (novella)
A CHARMING WISH

A CHARMING SPELL
A CHARMING MAGIC
A CHARMING SECRET
A CHARMING CHRISTMAS (novella)
A CHARMING FATALITY
A CHARMING DEATH (novella)
A CHARMING GHOST
A CHARMING HEX
A CHARMING VOODOO
A CHARMING CORPSE
A CHARMING MISFORTUNE
A CHARMING BLEND (CROSSOVER WITH A KILLER COFFEE COZY)
A CHARMING DECEPTION

Mail Carrier Cozy Mystery Series

Welcome to Sugar Creek Gap where more than the mail is being delivered.

STAMPED OUT
ADDRESS FOR MURDER
ALL SHE WROTE
RETURN TO SENDER
FIRST CLASS KILLER
POST MORTEM
DEADLY DELIVERY
RED LETTER SLAY

About Tonya

Tonya has written over 100 novels, all of which have graced numerous bestseller lists, including the USA Today. *Best known for stories charged with emotion and humor and filled with flawed characters, her novels have garnered reader praise and glowing critical reviews. She lives with her husband and a very spoiled rescue cat named Ro. Tonya grew up in the small southern Kentucky town of Nicholasville. Now that her four boys are grown men, Tonya writes full-time in her camper she calls her SHAMPER (she-camper).*

Learn more about her be sure to check out her website tonyakappes.com. Find her on Facebook, Twitter, BookBub, and Instagram

Sign up to receive her newsletter, where you'll get free books, exclusive bonus content, and news of her releases and sales.

If you liked this book, please take a few minutes to leave a review now! Authors (Tonya included) really appreciate this, and it helps draw more readers to books they might like. Thanks!

Cover artist: Mariah Sinclair: The Cover Vault

This book is a work of fiction. The characters, incidents, and dialogue are drawn from the author's imagination and are not to be construed as real. Any resemblance to actual events or persons, living or dead, is entirely coincidental. *Cover artist: Mariah Sinclair: The Cover Vault. Editor Red Adept.*

Copyright © 2023 by Tonya Kappes. All rights reserved. Printed in the United States of America. No part of this book may be used or reproduced in any manner whatsoever without written permission except in the case of brief quotations embodied in critical articles and reviews. For information email Tonyakappes@tonyakappes.com

Made in the USA
Las Vegas, NV
13 November 2024

11769808R00095